MW01470028

THE ILLITERATE DAUGHTER

Young Guardian Book One

CHIA GOUNZA VANG

©Copyright The Illiterate Daughter Chia Gounza Vang 2021

All rights reserved. No part of this publication may be reproduced, stored in a retrieval system, or transmitted, in any form or by any means without the prior written permission of the author, nor be otherwise circulated in any form of binding or cover other than that in which it is published and without a similar condition being imposed on the subsequent purchaser.

This is a work of fiction. Names, characters, places, and incidents are either the product of the author's imagination or are used fictitiously, and any resemblance to actual persons living or dead, business establishments, events, or locales, is entirely coincidental.

ISBN: Amazon 9798759203278

Cover design by dreams2media

First Trade Paperback Printing by Scarsdale Publishing, Ltd November 2021

10 9 8 7 6 5 4 3 2

If you purchased this book without a cover, you should be aware that this book is stolen property. It was reposted as "unsold and destroyed" to the publisher, and neither the author nor the publisher has received any payment for this "stripped book."

Cover Design by dreams2media

Editor: Rebecca Taverner Coleman

For Xang, Kalia, Zhia and Kung

My uncles who died in combat: Cher Pao Vang, Yeng Lee, and Wa Thao Yang.

My cousins who died in combat: Khwb Vang and Soua Vang.

All Hmong who died defending Laos.

My father, Wa Tong Vang, who was shot in the leg during the war. The wound in his leg continued to swell and caused him much pain until his death in 2017.

Foreword

Dear Readers,

Thank you for reading this book. I hope our story gives you insights into the Hmong's fight alongside the Americans, their flight from persecution by the communists to freedom in America, and their struggles and culture. While the Illiterate Daughter is a work of fiction, it is inspired by true events and contains real experiences of both my and my husband's family. I did love stories and was illiterate like the main character. I didn't get my education until I arrived in the United States. I loved learning and studied hard. Learning English as a second language was a challenge. I never imagined that one day I would be an author, but here I am. I appreciate your support and hope you will read the second book, Dreamer's Dream.

Chia Gounza Vang

Acknowledgments

A huge thank you to my beloved mother-in-law, Chao Lor Lee, who opened my eyes to my family's past about my people, my culture, and the Secret War. Because we shared a roof, she spent many hours telling me the tragedies that happened to her family and relatives. Her stories inspired me to learn more about the war. Although she passed away, her stories live on. She was one of the best mothers-in-law in the world. Her love for me and my children was as huge as the oceans, and I can never thank her enough.

Thank you to my mother, Xao Yang, brother-in-law, Cha Tou Lee, and others who shared their stories of fleeing the war. The stories along with my research and personal experiences enabled me to portray as best as I could an accurate picture of the situation in Laos at the time.

The people who helped me with this book in the early drafts are my brother Noah Vang and my friend Cathy Staeven. Noah and Cathy read, edited, and gave valuable suggestions. My friends Evelyn Hobbs and author Amanda Lauer read the manuscript. My colleagues Maryjo Pritzl proofread the first chapter of each revision and Ann Shover gave me encouragement and helped with sentence structures when needed. For the later drafts, my niece Bea Vang proofread and gave suggestions. They give me confidence and assurance to pursue publishing. Thank you.

The person who shaped my writing and the manuscript is my amazing mentor and teacher, Leykn Schmatz. Without Leykn, the manuscript would not have gotten to my publisher, Scarsdale. Meeting her was a blessing because she read, line edited, and gave valuable suggestions to the original version submitted to Scarsdale Publishing. She is the most influential person in my writing career. She is my hero. Thank you for all you have done for me, Leykn.

Thank you to my editors, Rebecca Coleman and Sharona Wilhelm, and the team at Scarsdale for making the book great. I couldn't have asked for a better publishing home.

Thank you to my children and husband for being patient with me and supportive. Their encouragement gave me courage and strength.

Terms

- Baht: Thai currency
- Hu plig: a soul calling ritual
- Kuam: a shaman's spiritual tool made of bull horn
- Niam tij: older sister-in-law
- Nyab: a daughter-in-law
- Paj ntaub: flowery cloth that describes appliqué, reverse appliqué, batik, cross stitch, and embroidery
- Qeej: a musical instrument consisting of six bamboo reeds
- Silver bar: currency used by the Hmong in Laos
- Tis nyab: a sister-in-law

Chapter One

May 1974

THE SUN ROASTED ME, AND MY SWEAT-STAINED, RAGGED, BLACK clothes clung and itched as I hoed weeds in my family's rice field. Two blisters had popped on my dirty palms and the raw skin hurt. The cramping pain in my back and hands surged with each slam and drag of my hoe. I dropped the hoe, straightened, and groaned.

I longed to be in a classroom. If the foolish war stopped, I could escape my family's backbreaking labor. I dreamed of learning stories about the universe, magic, demons, princes, and princesses. As usual, my musing eased my pain.

A crow cawed and snapped me out of my daydreams. I looked for Mother and caught sight of her across the field. She had assigned each of us a strip of field, and I had fallen far behind her. I'd needed the break, but my mother's scolds frightened me.

I scanned for Father and my sister, Der. They'd been more than halfway to the top of the hill and the end of the field but now were nowhere in sight. Neither was Der's boyfriend, Pheng. Der and Pheng had been hoeing side by side ahead of my parents. Weeding was intense work, and Pheng had helped Der for three days in a row. Where were they?

As I scanned the woods beyond the field, something swished near me. A bullet? I jumped back, heart racing. Instead of a bullet, a black crow landed on my shoulder. Its flutter tickled my cheek. I froze in shock. Then its sharp claws loosened their grip, and the crow flew away as fast as it had come.

My pounding heart slowed, then sank with new fear. The elders said that wild birds entering the home or landing on people were bad omens. What did this mean for me and my family? Tree stumps scattered the field. Why had the crow chosen to land on me instead of one of them? I might not be the best worker or a perfect daughter, but I hadn't done anything bad. I shivered despite the heat, and suddenly my knees gave way. I slumped on the dirt, head spinning.

Up ahead, Father limped out of the woods, headed in my direction. His right leg was shorter than the left, a result of the gunshot wound that ended his fighting with the Americans. Occasionally, the old injury would swell, and he'd have to walk with a stick. The war had made life hard for everyone.

Dangling at Father's side was a barong machete in a wooden case, fastened at his waist with a tied rope. His secret document was hidden inside the knife's bamboo handle, so he carried the knife everywhere.

As he drew near, Father said, "Nou, you look pale. Are you all right?"

If I told Father about the crow, he'd tell Mother, and she'd become frightened. Mother worried about everything.

"Yes." I took a deep breath to steady the quaver in my voice. "My back hurts, so I'm taking a short break."

"Don't take too long. Your mother will not be happy."

Father started across the field toward Mother. He worked

hard despite his short leg and never complained. Both my parents were far ahead of me on their work.

"Father," I called, "do you think the Communists will find our village?"

"I hope not," he replied without turning.

Since the departure of the American bombing crew, adults had whispered among themselves about the Communists invading villages. What was our chance of winning the war without the Americans? Losing the war would mean torture and enslavement instead of school. Anxious dread settled in my belly.

I prayed softly, "My honorable grandfather and ancestors, please protect us and our village from the Communist Pathet Lao. Protect our soldiers so that we win the war."

"Nou, get to work!" Mother yelled. "Stop daydreaming. You are so behind."

"I'm just taking a short break," I called back.

"You take too many breaks. Work harder to get your area weeded."

Anger burst inside me, and my sharp tongue slipped into disrespect and disobedience. "How come you don't make the boys work? Why do they get to stay home? It's not fair."

"You're good at complaining." Mother scowled and strode toward me.

She had told me that she yelled because she loved me, but her anger frightened me. Slowly, I stood, picked up the hoe, and returned to my work. When I was young, she spanked me for not completing my tasks. I was her naughtiest child. I tried to behave better and, as I grew older, she mostly scolded.

"Nou, you rushed through this." She pointed toward my toes, where a cluster of weeds lay covered in dirt. "Go back and get every weed out."

There were too many weeds. What she wanted was impossible, but I wouldn't win by arguing and couldn't show more disrespect.

I sighed loudly. "All right."

"Do it right the first time or do it over." Mother shook her head. "You have a lot to learn, my daughter. You need to work hard like your sister. Skills are important for your life. Stories and books are not, so don't waste your time daydreaming."

I flared my nostrils in anger. It was true I daydreamed, but I hated when Mother compared me to Der, who was patient, reliable, and obedient. Comparing and scolding were meant to make me work harder, but they drained my enthusiasm and energy. They lowered my self-esteem because I would never be like my sister. I was born different. My dreams were full of folklore and curiosity about the universe, not physical work. I hated myself for my lack of motivation to be a hard worker and a perfect daughter. I hated the war, and I hated my sister and mother for refusing to help me. How could I be self-sufficient if they didn't have the patience to teach me?

"Get to work." Mother, petite but strong, walked steadily back toward her area.

"Mother, is Der taking a break?" I asked.

"Yes."

"Why aren't you yelling at her?"

"Pheng and Der got a lot done," Mother shouted over her shoulder.

I bit my lip. Before Der began dating Pheng, she and I worked together, supporting and helping each other. Der's assistance had declined since, and her excuse was that I had to learn to be independent. Now, she ignored me because of her annoying boyfriend, who came around whenever he wanted. Proper courting took place in the evening, but Pheng wanted to show off his skills to impress my parents. His help was changing Der, making her lazy and undependable. If he wasn't present, Der would have checked on me and asked how I was doing.

I dropped the hoe and headed to nearby trees. Pheng and Der sat shoulder to shoulder in the shade, their hands entwined. Wind soughed through the branches. Pheng turned to Der and kissed her cheek.

Disgusted, I shouted, "Don't you do that to my sister!"

Pheng shot me a worried glance. "I love your sister. A kiss is all right. You can ask her."

I looked down, regretting my sharp, loud voice.

Der's dimples appeared on her thin, fair-skinned face. She kissed Pheng on the cheek. "Someday, you'll know what love is."

How dare she shame the family by kissing a man in front of others? I clapped my hand over my mouth to suppress a scolding. I couldn't scold her because Der had been my second mother since our twin brothers were born, and I relied on her for everything. Wasn't she ashamed of herself? Our parents had high expectations for her, a perfect daughter. Maybe she wasn't perfect, after all.

I flicked a glance at Pheng. Heat flushed my body. Disrespecting a guest was shameful, so I took a deep breath and walked away, head low and shoulders slumped. Der's and the crow's strange behaviors fueled my stress. I wished to remain a child and to be a son, so I'd have freedom like my brothers.

Nearing my weeding area, I stretched my back and scanned the rich, green, knee-high rice plants that stretched across the rolling hills and swayed in the breeze. In far off fields, other villagers bent over patches of land, tending to their livelihoods. It was now May, the month my sister and I were born. The crops and harvesting seasons helped me know where we were in time. Thirteen summers had passed since I came into the world. My family had been fleeing war since I was seven. Three summers ago, Father gave me two Laotian books and promised me I could go to school when we won the war. I yearned for school.

Mid-afternoon, my family stopped weeding. Pheng picked his way carefully around the rice plants to Father, who lingered nearby. They shook hands.

"Thank you for your help again today," Father said in a bubbly voice.

Pheng's mouth quirked into a smile. The dirt that encrusted his face made him look older than eighteen. His black, wide-legged trousers and black shirt were stained with mud.

"It was my pleasure. Thanks for allowing me to be with Der," Pheng said.

"It's hard work. If you don't mind, you are welcome to come every day."

"I'll be back tomorrow," Pheng replied.

Pheng didn't mind the hard work because he got to kiss Der. Who wouldn't want to be with a beautiful girl like Der? I was happy to see him go.

Later, in the vegetable patch, Der and I picked gai choy. A cool breeze brushed my long face and tousled a strand of hair into my eyes.

Der dropped a handful of gai choy in the rattan basket and stood. "Get up and I'll fix your hair for the evening chores. I don't want your hair in our food."

I brushed dirt off my black trousers, tightened the red and green sashes around my waist, and stood with my back to Der. She removed a metal barrette clip, and my long hair fell on my shoulders. My sister gathered the loose strands and started braiding. Having Der by my side, my back pain and the crow faded from my mind.

"I love your silky hair and big round eyes." Der's voice was soft and gentle.

"You just say that to make me feel better."

"Soften your voice," she said. "I want to tell you a secret."

"A secret?"

"You can't tell anyone, especially our parents."

Der quickly wove my hair and clipped it with the barrette. Then, she untied a small, black drawstring bag that dangled from her red sash. She took out a beautiful silver ring in the shape of a kite elaborated with small triangles.

"What kind of ring is this?" I asked.

"It's called *Nplhaib Kooj Nplias*."

The name meant "grasshopper," but the ring didn't look like a grasshopper. "How did you get it?"

"Pheng gave me the ring. It is his promised gift to me." Joy filled her voice. "Although we've been dating for only three months, it was love at first sight. We are going to get married soon."

My heart almost jumped out of my chest. "No! Don't leave me!"

"Quiet!" Der whispered. "Why do you always talk so loud? I don't want Mother and Father to hear us."

I softened my voice, "Why?"

"I don't want our parents to know about this." Her voice was quiet but rough. "It's embarrassing. They will find out when I'm at Pheng's home and his family notifies them that Pheng and I are married. I'm sharing the news with you in advance because you are my sister and my best friend."

I recalled my friend Maineng saying that her sister had married in secrecy. Her brother-in-law took her sister to his home one night. The marriage was announced after her parents were notified. This was a tradition that the majority of couples practiced.

It was nice of Der to share her secret, but her news weighed heavily. I sank to the weeds. Der sat with me shoulder to shoulder.

"I'm only getting married. Nothing to worry about," she said.

"I'm going to miss you, and I won't have free time to listen to Aunty Shoua's stories anymore," I cried. "And I can't cook. Mother will scold me more."

"You haven't learned to soften your voice. Try harder."

I scowled.

"Mother can tell you her stories," Der said.

"I've heard all her stories." I grasped Der's hand. "You are only sixteen. You should wait until you are older."

"It's love. Pheng and I are ready to marry."

I knew there was no way I could convince her to wait. Suddenly cold, I hugged my knees and imagined the misery I'd face, burdened with all the chores and without her help. And the loneliness. My chest heaved in sadness. After a long silence, I drew a deep breath.

I steadied my voice and said, "When are you leaving?"

"In two days, because that's the auspicious date Pheng's father wants us to have. Don't tell anyone and ruin my marriage."

"I won't," I whispered.

The prettiest girl and the handsomest boy in the village were getting married, and I was losing my sister. I hoped the crow had come to warn me of that loss. I hoped there wasn't more bad luck.

Chapter Two

THE SUN, A BLISTERING RED SPHERE OF LIGHT, DWINDLED beneath the western horizon. Like many others, my family trudged home to our village, Thao. My parents knew all fifty families residing here. Thao was a quiet, peaceful place, and we loved it. Mountains surrounded us on four sides, shielding us from the enemy and giving me a sense of security. Nonresidents wouldn't know a village existed. Brown thatch huts were scattered throughout the small valley with our hut on the north side near the woods.

As we passed the Vue's hut, our closest neighbor, our roosters crowed, their squawk welcoming me home. Nothing felt better than coming to the place I loved. Our hut, made of bamboo walls and an elephant grass roof, stood before us.

My eight-year-old twin brothers, Tong and Hlao, squealed as they rushed past Der and me to meet our parents. Hlao grabbed Father's arm and Tong grabbed Mother's. The boys spoke rapidly about their small-game snare traps. At the fire pit, they showed our parents four birds on the ground. Mother and Father's eyes gleamed, and they praised my brothers with enthusiasm for their ingenuity.

Standing near the fire pit, I crossed my arms and stared at them. The boys were praised for having fun while I was scolded for working hard. Since Mother demanded that I master all the skills expected for a wife, I had been working extra hard to be like my perfect sister. My parents weren't fair, and I wanted to tell them that but was afraid of more scolding. They seemed to have no hope in me, a useless girl. My life was difficult as an unattended middle child and an imperfect daughter.

The boys squealed and pulled our parents to sit with them by the fire pit. They talked about making traps in the woods and playing at the duck pond with our big brother, Toua.

I envied my brothers. I truly missed the fun time I had babysitting the twins three years ago. When I turned ten, my mother said I was old enough for other work and prohibited me from playing with them. I became Grandmother's caretaker, and I helped with farm work and chores.

My ninety-year-old grandmother was absent from the group, but her snores emanated from her bed. I went to her bamboo cot enclosed with a gray cloth on two sides. Only she and my parents had fabrics enclosing their beds. Grandmother lay on her side. I touched her scrawny hand. It felt cold. I covered her with a blanket. She relied on the family for everything, especially me, but I liked helping her because she told me stories and never scolded me.

My brother Toua came in, carrying an ax. He was two years older than Der and tall and lean with a strong forehead and jaw. He had just finished splitting logs outside. Toua set the ax against the bamboo wall by the door.

"Toua and I are going to a meeting with the neighbors," said Father. "We'll be back."

"I want to go with you," Hlao said.

"You can go with me when you are older."

Father and Toua left for the meeting.

Der and I rested on our bamboo cot to catch our breath. Like always, I reached beneath the bed for the bamboo box that contained my treasures. I pulled out one of the books, then turned it over to admire the cover.

"When are you going to stop touching that book?" asked Der.

"When I can read and know its story."

I turned the pages. The book gave me hope. One day I'd be able to go to school and read it. How long would it take to learn how to read Hmong or Lao? Unfamiliar with Lao, it would be more difficult to learn, but I would study hard.

"It's time for chores." Der stood.

I huffed. "Can we rest longer?"

"No time."

I sighed. I had to obey my master, so I placed the book back in the box and shoved it under the bed. While Der cooked, I fetched water and fed the chickens and pigs.

During supper, Der ate quickly, then disappeared outside without a word. Concerned, I followed her and found her vomiting into the brown dirt.

Panic spread through my nerves. "What's wrong?" I wrapped an arm around Der's shoulder. "I'll have Mother give you herbal medicine."

"I'm all right." Der wiped the back of her hand across her mouth. "I'm just having an upset stomach. I'm all better now." She shook my arm from her shoulders. "Go inside."

I hesitated, then said, "If you say so."

Inside, I helped my grandmother to her cot and tucked her in. Then I cleaned the dining area quickly, so I wouldn't be late for story time.

Our black ridgeback dog, Fox, curled up by the front door. I smoothed his back and said, "Go."

He got up, and we snuck out the door. He hunted and guarded us, so we fed him well, making him heavy but muscular. Fox was my bodyguard during the night when I had to relieve myself or go somewhere. I felt safe with him leading me. We found our way by moonlight to Aunty Shoua's home, five huts away. Her booming voice echoed from the backyard. The fire pit gave warmth and light to the group. As I joined the circle of four, Fox lay down nearby. Maineng, my friend, hurried in and sat next to me.

Aunty Shoua, the storyteller, said, "You are lazy! You can't do anything right! Get out!"

She was telling the story of an orphan boy. His mean sister-in-law was kicking him out. This part was interesting and, though I had heard it a few times, the storyteller's skill and having my friend by my side were a comfort. I was thankful to have my parents. Otherwise, I'd be like the orphan boy.

Suddenly, Der appeared out of the darkness. "Nou, go home. You have to finish your chores."

Aunty Shoua stopped, and everyone's eyes were on me. My cheeks grew hot, and anger shot through my gut, but I couldn't argue in front of the group.

"Can you finish them for me please?" I begged.

"You must come home with me now," Der ordered.

What was wrong her? Der had become a mean sister since dating Pheng. Maybe she wanted me to hate her, so I wouldn't miss her when she left.

I sighed heavily. "Maineng, I'll see you tomorrow night."

"Yes, see you tomorrow," said Maineng. "Finish your chores before you come. I want you to stay longer."

I nodded.

On the way home, I said, "Der, does getting married mean you won't help me anymore?"

"No one is going to help you after I leave. Stories will not help you with your life."

Mother said that, too, but the stories did help me with my life. They relieved my anxiety, and they helped me understand a world beyond the drudgery of chores and backbreaking work. Why couldn't Mother and Der understand? I quickened my pace with Fox.

At home, I washed the dishes, removed ashes from the mud stove, and went to bed. Der came later, and her tossing and turning annoyed me. I put the blanket I used as a pillow between us, then I fell asleep.

I awoke to a hand on my shoulder, shaking me. I pushed it away. "Stop it, Der. I'm tired."

"Get up," she ordered. "Quickly! The Communists are burning homes."

I snapped my eyes open, heart racing. I kicked off the blanket and jumped to my feet, then peered through a gap in the bamboo wall of the thatch hut. Flames and smoke filled the night sky. The homes in the south burned. I stood in shock, trembling, my arms wrapped across my chest.

Der tugged at my shoulder. "Come on!"

The little boys whined, and Mother hushed them. Toua and I rushed out first followed by Der and Mother, who each carried a twin on her back. Father limped behind us carrying my grandmother. The fierce fire lightened the dark night sky. In the south, gunshots snapped through the village, and people screamed for help. Fear squeezed the breath out of me. I prayed to my ancestors.

We rushed past the pigpen, where suddenly I halted. I'd left my books in the hut. I couldn't live without them. As I debated the risk of going back, I realized I'd lost track of my family. I looked wildly around, heart hammering. The fire hadn't reached our hut and I saw no sign of the enemy. My dream overpowered my fear.

I raced back toward our home. A gust of wind swept past and shoved me to the ground. I landed on my knees. Pain shot up my legs. Adrenaline coursed through my veins. The village spun around me.

Fox barked ferociously. He slept outside the front door, and Father had forgotten him. My desperation to save the dog and my books forced me to my feet through pain and fear. As I ran, glowing embers sparked everywhere, catching more thatch huts on fire. Gasping for air and trembling, I stumbled and fell again. Gunshots erupted, and Fox's barking stopped. My heart stopped, too. I remained on the ground, afraid to move.

"Heaven, no," I whimpered.

Sobbing, I hit the rough earth with my fist. The attack had happened so fast. Our hunter and bodyguard was gone. I had known Fox for seven years, since he was a puppy, and couldn't imagine life without him. Anger and grief burst inside me. I wanted to scream and cry, calling on Earth and Heaven to punish evil people, but I choked back my sobs, trying to stay quiet so the soldiers wouldn't kill me, too.

"Nou, where are you?" Der called.

"Over here." Gunshots and fire surrounded us. "Over here!" I shouted.

Der ran toward me, and I pushed to a sitting position. Many times, when I had nightmares, Der, who slept beside me, would wake me to tell me that I was dreaming and everything was all right. I could only wish this was a dream. Der yanked me to my feet. I leaned on her for support as we rushed to our wooden pigpen on the north side near the peach orchard.

As soon as we reached the concealment of the pigpen fence, I asked softly, "Where's everyone?"

"Mother, the twins, and Toua are by the peach orchard," said Der, breathlessly. "I don't know where Father and Grandmother are."

Our hut began to burn, and my heart stopped a second time. My books! Oh Heaven! I turned my head away and clung to Der. I tried to swallow my grief, but it was too strong, and tears burst out of me like the smoke. Der pulled me against her, my face on her chest, and she stroked my hair. Our dog, my books, and everything we had worked for, gone in the blink of an eye. Three years ago, we came here because our lives were in danger, but that danger had been nothing like this.

Through the fence, in the light of the fire, I saw the enemy herding a large group of villagers to the woods. Father and Grandmother? Dread swirled in my belly, and my limbs shook. Der shook, too. I prayed. We huddled together as we waited for the Communist Pathet Lao to leave. It seemed like years.

Finally, the group disappeared into the forest.

"Let's look for Father and Grandmother," I urged.

She shook her head. "It's not safe. Some of the Communist soldiers are still in the village."

"If they are, we must get Father and Grandmother out of here. Hurry!" I cried.

Der hesitated, then asked, "Can you walk?"

My knees hurt, my head spun, my heart ached, and my vision blurred, but I had no choice. "I have to."

We crouched and hugged the shadows as we ran to the chicken coop.

Der called softly, "Father?"

"Under the coop," Father answered.

I breathed a sigh of relief. He and Grandmother crawled out. I was so happy to see them safe that I didn't care how awful they smelled. I threw my arms around my grandmother's shoulders. She trembled as badly as I did.

"We're all right," I whispered.

She sobbed. I didn't know what to say, so I smoothed her hair.

"Father, are you all right?" I asked.

"Yes," he whispered. "Where are the others?"

"By the peach orchard," Der whispered.

"Thank our ancestors everyone is safe," he said. "Having our home near the woods saved us."

At the peach orchard, our family reunited in the darkness beneath the trees.

"Is everyone all right?" Father asked.

"Yes," Mother whispered.

The heartache and dread that still swirled in my belly made me want to touch each of them, to feel everyone's life and make sure they were unharmed. I reached for my twin brothers' hands. They were cold, but the boys squeezed my fingers. Knowing Toua wouldn't like his hand touched, I patted his shoulder. He brushed my hand off.

"What are you doing?" he asked.

"Just checking," I said, and my tension eased a bit.

Father led us deeper into the woods, picking his way around logs and vines where the trees shielded us. We gathered on the far side of a giant tree that would conceal us from view.

Cold, exhausted and achy, I tucked myself against my sister for warmth and comfort. Der wrapped her arms around me to give me heat. The twins were bundled together on Mother's lap next to us.

"Nou, are you all right?" Mother whispered.

"I fell, but I'm all right."

I lied because I didn't want Mother to worry. My knees hurt. My dreams were shattered. I was physically and emotionally wounded, but I wanted to keep that knowledge to myself.

My family sat in silence, as we stared at the distant flames that billowed up into the dark sky. No one dared to make any noise. My legs shook.

Did that crow bring a warning? Or had it led the Communists to us?

Chapter Three

As the sun climbed higher into the sky, the woods glowed. Father had been pacing for a long time.

"Toua's going with me to search for survivors," he said. "The rest of you stay put."

"Father, I want to go, too," I said softly. The Communists had taught me to lower my voice at last, and the death of our dog made me love and appreciate the people around me. "I want to look for Maineng, Aunty Shoua, and their families."

"No. You'd be scared," said Toua. Being a son and the oldest child, he thought he was in charge.

"I'll be fine," I shot back.

"It's not safe," Father said.

If I were a son, Father would have allowed me. I could try to persuade him like I did in the past but knew he wouldn't relent.

Der stared at me. "You are not going anywhere. I can't believe you risked your life for those useless books."

I hung my head. No one understood my love of stories. Der didn't understand my shattered dreams. I loved Der but wondered what it would be like to have a sister who cared about what mattered to me.

Father and Toua left. I hoped Maineng, Aunty Shoua, and their families were safe. I wished to cross paths with them soon. Grandmother coughed. As she leaned on a tree trunk, fear clouded her features.

I brushed away the pieces of chicken manure that stained her gray hair.

"Grandmother, I'm sorry that you have to go through this."

Her eyes brimmed with tears. "Don't worry about me, and don't lose hope. You're young. Be strong."

I held her wrinkled, cold hands in mine. Instead of stroking her hair to show my love, as was our custom, I said, "I love you, Grandmother." In the folk tales, the characters showed love by telling each other. I liked that better.

Her expression softened. "I love you, too."

We waited anxiously for Father and Toua to return. Every sound and shadow felt like the enemy.

When the sun hung high above the tree canopy, Father and Toua finally returned.

"All fifty huts were burned to ashes." Father's eyes were wet. "The thirty silver bars that we hid under our bed are gone. The enemy probably searched every hut before setting them on fire."

My pulse accelerated. I put my head in my hands, wondering if the people managed to escape the fire and the shooting.

"That's our life savings." Mother buried her face in her hands.

Tong and Hlao, who each clung to her, whimpered with fright. Mother pulled them onto her lap. She shook with sobs. It was the first time I saw my mother unable to control her emotions.

A fire burned inside me. The war had robbed us of everything. I stroked Mother's hair. It was the only thing I could offer. Now we had nothing but the clothes we wore. How long would they last?

"We didn't find anyone." Father's voice wavered. "They fled the area, were captured, or killed."

Terror flashed across Der's face. I reached for her hands. She trembled. She didn't know if Pheng was dead or alive. I hadn't wanted her to get married and leave. Now I wanted them to be together. Having lost my books and Fox, I knew how losing something you loved felt. Der clapped a hand against her mouth to stifle her sobs.

"I'm sorry, Der." I wrapped my arms around her. If Pheng and his family escaped, Der had a chance.

"We'll go to the rice field to gather some rice and the cooking pots that we stored there," said Father. "We'll be on our way to a safe place." He touched the barong machete in its wooden case, which dangled from the rope tied around his waist. "Good thing I grabbed this last night."

The knife was Father's precious weapon. It carried an important document in its bamboo tube handle. A round, smooth wooden peg was inserted to block the tube and to hold the handle in place. Thin bamboo strings were wound around the handle to keep it from splitting. No one could guess the secrets hidden inside the handle. Everyone had secrets. The war itself was called The Secret War.

"Father, is the attack a sign that the Communist Pathet Lao are winning the war?" I asked.

"It looks like it, but I still have hope." Father was hesitant. "The Hmong soldiers are doing everything they can without the Americans."

I didn't want to believe we could lose. "Tell me about the Americans on your list."

Father took out the paper hidden inside the handle of his barong machete. He unfolded it and pointed to a name. "This is CIA Jerry Daniels. He trains the Hmong troops in Long Chieng and is also a military advisor to General Vang Pao. The Americans all have big noses and big blue eyes with skin as pale as the moon. They like to hug people, and they are fun." Father cleared his throat. "One night, Jerry brought some rice wine to cheer us up. We drank with him and stayed up until midnight. Jerry and his Hmong interpreter, Lo Ma, told us about America. That night, we learned more about democracy, and we learned that it is important to keep a paper trail of our involvement in the war."

"Is that why you have the list of the American names?" I asked.

"This paper not only has the American names but my record of fighting. This is the proof that I fought in the war. I have to keep it safe."

"Very important paper," Mother whispered.

What is democracy? I started to ask, but Father stood.

"We are leaving now. Get ready," he said.

Father put the paper back in its hiding place in the handle of his machete, then helped Grandmother to her feet. A few birds sang loudly. I wondered if they were cheering us or warning us of what was ahead. I felt a crushing pain in my chest as we had to abandon the fields. As much as I hated weeding, I hated more to see our work go to waste.

I whacked a nearby tree with a stick I found. "I hate you, Communists! I hate you, bastards!"

Der seized my arm, and I dropped the stick. We walked on together.

Chapter Four

WE WERE ON OUR WAY TO A SAFE PLACE.

Midday approached. Father carried Grandmother on his back. Der walked even more slowly, causing the two of us to fall behind. She had thrown up her breakfast and barely had energy to move. She stopped, dropped her rattan basket in the middle of the narrow, overgrown trail, and slumped on the grass.

I took the rice for our lunch from her basket and put it in mine. "You are not carrying anything now," I said. "Can we go?"

"I need rest," said Der, breathlessly.

I glanced at my family who weren't too far ahead. Der's slow pace would hinder us. I wanted to tell her to get up, but she softly cried, and pain etched her features. I couldn't use my loud voice to call to my family, so I ran to catch up with them.

"Mother, Der needs to rest," I said, out of breath.

They stopped, and Mother and Father exchanged a look.

"All right," said Mother. "We will rest and eat lunch."

I set my basket against a tree and took out the pot of rice and banana leaves.

Mother gave each person a ration of rice on a leaf. I took

my ration and Der's and returned to where she still sat. I tried to coax her to take a few small bites, but she only shook her head. At last, Mother came over.

"Eat," Mother ordered. "You need energy to walk and fight your illness."

Der stared at the rice and ate a little but couldn't keep it down. Mother studied her closely. Der's face was as pale as the moon. Mother's soft features hardened and her eyes narrowed.

Puzzled, I looked from Mother to Der and back to Mother. "What's the matter?"

"I'm so sorry, Mother." Der wrung her hands in her lap. "I'm ashamed."

"Your Father, where would he hide his face?" Mother's voice was thick with mortification. "Why do you let us down?"

Der hung her head. "I'm sorry."

"Didn't I tell you not to have sex until you are married?" Mother demanded.

"Yes." Der's voice wobbled. "Pheng and I love each other, and we were going to get married."

"You're pregnant?" I asked in disbelief.

Der nodded. Everything made sense now. Pheng knew Der was pregnant. That was why he spent time helping her with everything. I bit my bottom lip, turned away, and shut my eyes in anguish. Being pregnant without marriage was a disgrace. Der would be the first girl in the village to have a child out of wedlock. She was no longer the perfect daughter, and I hated Pheng, and I hated the war. Mother always said to me, *"Be like your sister and do what she does."* Would she say that now?

"Did Pheng know you are pregnant with his child?" Mother demanded.

Der nodded. "That was why we planned to get married."

Mother reached for Der's ear, and impulsively I swatted her hand away. She used to twist my ears for my disobedience. Mother glared like a tiger about to attack.

"I'm sorry, Mother," I said. I didn't mean to hit her. I knew all mothers spanked their naughty kids. But my instinct to protect Der, like she had defended me many times before, had taken over. "Der apologized for not listening to you. This is her first time."

Mother didn't slap me as expected. Instead, she turned to my sister. "Der, I'm angry because I love you. If we can't find Pheng, your reputation will be ruined. You won't find a decent husband. You are so beautiful. You deserve a handsome, decent husband. Why didn't you listen to me?"

"I know you want the best for me, and I'm sorry," Der whispered. "Father won't love me anymore for bringing shame to the family."

"We are on our way to a new village," I said. "If anyone asks, we can say there was an attack and Der's husband is missing. No one will know."

"That will only hide her shame. She's no longer a virgin. A handsome, decent man won't want her." Mother looked at me. "Nou, you are still obsessed with learning, but soon you will like boys. You must know that you should never have sex until you are married. Your husband is the only one who sees your body. Do you understand?"

I nodded. "Yes."

Father walked over. "Are you all right, Der?"

Der looked at Mother. Shame clouded Mother's features. "Wa Shoua, Der's having morning sickness. She's pregnant with Pheng's baby. They were going to get married, but the attack happened. I'm so sorry for her disgraceful behavior."

"I'm sorry, Father," cried Der.

Father shook his head. "I have high expectations for you and Nou. For a beautiful girl like you, I expect your future husband to ask my permission to marry you."

"Father, it's not Der's fault," I blurted. "It's Pheng's fault! He's older. I'm sure he forced her."

"Hush before the Communists find us," Mother hissed.

Father's eyes shimmered with tears. He turned and walked away with drooping shoulders. Mother followed without asking me and Der to come along. My parents' disappointment cut like a knife. Der burst into tears. I extended my long sleeve to wipe her tears, but she brushed my hand off. Her sorrow pained me.

"Father is angry, but I know he loves you," I said. "I love you no matter what."

She squeezed her eyes shut.

"Everything will be all right. I won't let anyone hurt you," I said.

Der opened her eyes. "Very kind of you to prevent an ear pull, but there is nothing you can do."

"I don't have magic powers like the folklore heroes, but I can help you with anything you need. Don't give up hope. That orphan boy in Aunty Shoua's story suffered so much, but he found love, peace, and prosperity at the end."

Der dried her face with her long sleeves. "The storyteller has filled your brain with fiction."

Getting Der to dry her eyes and speak made my chest swell with pride. "I think the universe is full of mysteries. This is why I love stories and want to go to school to learn about facts and fiction."

"Thanks for talking to me." Der spoke in a brittle voice that frightened me. "I am blessed to have you. Now give me your arm. I need support."

I helped her to her feet, and we trudged after our family.

Chapter Five

For three days, we journeyed past two valleys, two mountains, and descended toward the third valley. The sun was low. Father pointed to a small village ahead. My pulse quickened, and I grabbed Der's arm. We glanced at each other with sparkling eyes. I couldn't wait to rest in a warm thatch hut. Since the attack, we had slept in the creepy forest. Finding a village gave me a sense of security.

The village was deserted. Knee-high weeds surrounded most of the flimsy thatch huts. A few huts were in good condition and seemed as though other travelers had used them for temporary shelters. My family settled into one of those.

Shortly after my parents left to forage for water and firewood, an unpleasant chill settled in the hut despite the warm sun. It was strange. Something about the hut felt wrong.

"Der, do you have a strange feeling about this hut?" I asked.

Der lay on the only bamboo cot with Grandmother. She looked around and shook her head. "No. It's fine to me."

At least she had answered. Since the attack, Der spoke less and cried often.

As the sun disappeared and the air cooled to match the chill that crawled over my skin, my eight-year-old brothers ran outside to play. The precious boys didn't get to walk much, so they were full of energy. I followed them because Mother had instructed me to keep an eye on them.

I sat on weeds and watched my small brothers play tag in an open space. Hlao, who had flat cheeks and a wider nose like Mother, mostly chased Tong, who had Father's long face and big nose. They soon got bored and reached for my hand to play hide-and-seek with them. I was the seeker and started counting while my brothers went to hide. After counting to ten, I went after them.

"Tong and Hlao, where are you?" The twins lay flat with their faces down in a patch of isolated grass. I pretended I didn't see them. "Where are you? I can't see you."

When I moved closer, they giggled loudly, and I was reminded of how free we had been before the Communists attacked.

The night closed in, and I put the twins to bed. The adults and I sat around the fire pit to keep warm. Father's pant legs were rolled up to his knees, and in the glow of the fire, his wounded leg was visible. There was no calf muscle on his right leg, only a huge scar the size of his fist that made standing on his right foot difficult.

"Father, your wound is big. You shouldn't go to war anymore," I said.

"Even if I want to, I can't fight anymore. I'm over sixty now, and my leg keeps me from being a soldier."

"Did you get paid for being a soldier?" I asked.

"Yes, about two dollars a month," he replied.

"Is that a lot?"

He shook his head.

"Who paid you?"

"The Americans paid and trained us to fight. With Laos as a neutral country, the Americans can only drop bombs on the enemy, so we fought the Communists on the battlefield."

"Why do you want to know everything?" Toua demanded. "Girls don't need to know war stuff."

"I have the right to know," I snapped.

Having Father there gave me the courage. He usually told me anything I wanted to know.

"The more you know, the more frightened you will be," my brother said. "Girls are scaredy-cats."

My pulse quickened. I was not a scaredy-cat.

Father put out the fire and said, "Go to sleep."

I helped Grandmother to the cot. Then I cuddled with her while everyone else settled on the dirt floor using banana leaves as mats.

A cry brought me bolt upright from sleep, heart hammering. I had no idea how long I had slept.

"Where does it hurt?" Mother asked in the darkness.

"Everywhere," Hlao murmured.

Usually, I stayed out of my parents' business, but the attack had changed me. I got up and picked my way in the dark to the fire pit. I put the half-burned firewood back into the pit, found a nearby match, and got the fire going. My parents brought the twins to the fire pit, and they each sat with a boy on their lap. Father covered Tong with his shirt, while Mother wrapped Hlao with a small, ragged, gray blanket from the hut. I peeked through the cracked bamboo wall to the outside. It was dark, midnight, and quiet. No sign of the Communists.

"The boys have chest pain." Mother sounded panicky. "Nou! Get the sack of herbal medicine and find the chest pain roots."

The bag had many jagged roots, and I didn't know which was which. My hands shook as I searched.

"Hurry!" Mother yelled.

"I'm trying."

"Just give me the bag!"

I thrust the bag toward Mother. I had failed her. She hastily sorted out a small bundle of dried roots.

"Boil some water," she ordered.

That I could do. Der got up to help, but I made her sit back down. Her morning sickness and depression had weakened her.

The boys weren't better after drinking the herbal medicine. They were now too ill to cry. My heart squirmed around in my chest, making me unable to sit still, so I paced the hut. For the first time, my love for the twins outweighed my envy.

Throughout the night, Father chanted and prayed, asking Lord of Heaven and our ancestors to heal the boys. Grandmother prayed many times, too. I boiled all kinds of herbal medicines. I was proud of myself for doing something.

When the sun climbed high, the twins vomited blood. My fear spiked, and being helpless, I cried. Grandmother stroked my hair, but her gesture didn't help. In a cracking voice, Mother begged Father to find a shaman, even though she knew there weren't any people or shamans in the vacant village. Father's exasperated look showed how helpless he felt. Mother kept asking for a shaman, her face blotchy and her eyes bloodshot.

I whispered to Grandmother, "Why does she want a shaman so badly?"

"Your mother's herbal medicines didn't work, so she thinks it must be evil spirits taking away the twins' souls."

I gasped, heart pounding. Were the devils sucking my brothers' blood before taking their souls like the stories I'd heard? In folklore, people used magic to counterattack devils.

"How are we going to save them?" I said in a wobbly voice.

"Only a shaman can resuscitate their souls so they can heal," Father replied.

"Father and Mother, we must find a shaman," I cried. "Toua and I can travel to find one."

Mother's eyes brightened. "Yes!"

"Where?" Toua said. "It'll take days to find a village. The boys need a shaman now."

Father's expression dulled. "There's nothing we can do."

His words stabbed my heart, and my stomach felt as hard as a stone. I sucked in several deep breaths. I'd do anything for my brothers, but how?

I smoothed their hair. "I love you! Please get better. We'll have so much fun together."

They didn't respond. Their faces were ashen with their eyes closed. Chills ran up my spine. I turned to Der and buried my head against her chest like a baby. We all prayed for a miracle. There was nothing else to do.

At noon, Hlao, the youngest twin, stopped breathing. His fingers loosened and dropped from Mother's shirt. Then Tong stopped breathing, too. Father held him tight. He and Mother screamed like they were being murdered.

Rage and grief flared through me, burning my insides. I screamed as loud as thunder to let Heaven and Earth hear my pain. Grandmother stroked my hair. Toua and Der wailed. Our cries echoed around the hut and out to the quiet village. For the moment, grief overpowered caution.

I screamed until my lungs gave out, then I collapsed near the fire pit. My throat hurt like hell. I was devastated when our dog was killed and my books were burned, but those experiences couldn't compare to this.

The hut remained quiet for what seemed a lifetime. Mother's eyes were red and puffy when she finally asked Father to let her hold Tong. She squeezed both twins on her lap and held their hands tightly. I scooted over to Mother and touched my brothers' hands. They had turned cold and stiff, but my mother wouldn't release them. Father wanted to bury them, but she refused.

The sun disappeared. There was nothing to cook, and we hadn't eaten anything all day. I was senseless with grief and felt no hunger, but I worried about Grandmother.

"Grandmother, are you hungry?" I asked in a small voice.

She shook her head. "If there is food, I won't be able to swallow it."

Mother still held the dead boys, as she stared at the bamboo wall, her eyes glassy and unfocused.

"Mother, are you hungry?" I asked.

My mother stared at me confused. She blinked, seeming to come back to us.

"My boys must be hungry." She shook them. "Wake up. Wake up."

They did not wake. My mother collapsed on the dirt floor with them.

I shrieked, "Mother! Are you all right?"

Heaven, I couldn't lose her. My heart leapt into my throat.

Father checked her pulse and lay her flat on the dirt. "She fainted. Don't worry. She'll be all right."

My heart gradually slowed. I sat by my mother as my father lifted the twins and placed the two small bodies in the dining area within the bamboo frame he'd made earlier. Der kept an eye on the twins and shooed flies from their bodies. Once Mother regained consciousness, she crawled to the boys.

"Wake up, my boys, wake up," she cried. "How am I going to live without you?" She blew her nose and rested her head on Hlao's stomach. "You were my hope and my life and now it's gone, gone forever. I am nothing now. My life is over."

Tears trickled down my cheeks. Sons were important, and losing the beloved twins was a tragedy, but Mother still had three children. Why would she say she was nothing and her life was over?

"I love you, Mother." I sat next to her. "I'm sorry for everything."

"I love you, too," Der said.

Mother grasped our hands and squeezed them tight.

My family stayed awake together through another night, as we mourned the dead boys.

Chapter Six

THE SUN CREPT OVER THE VILLAGE. I TRUDGED TO THE NEARBY creek. In the clear water I saw my reflection, puffy and red-eyed. I still couldn't believe the twins were gone. I hated the war. I hated everything that happened to my family. I kicked a nearby twig, sending it flying across the creek to crash into the trees. I closed my eyes and breathed deeply. Then I quickly filled my bamboo tube with water and hurried back. In the backyard, I washed my grandmother's face with my bare hand. I combed her gray hair with my fingers.

"Grandmother, it's tragic to have lost the twins, but I don't understand why my mother said her life was over."

"A woman who has no son is worthless and is a burden to the community," said Grandmother in a thin voice.

"But she has Toua."

Grandmother coughed. "Toua's not your mother's son."

"What?" I couldn't believe my ears. "What do you mean?"

"Your mother is not Toua's biological mother. His mother was your father's first wife."

My throat squeezed tight. I slowly sat down on the dirt. Why hadn't anyone told me? Were there other secrets? Now I understood why Mother always tended to the twins, fed them first at every meal and spoiled them by carrying them every day. They were her treasures, her protectors, her hope, and her future. No son meant no life. What would this mean for my mother's future?

"My mother can no longer give birth." My voice wavered with anguish. "Is my father going to marry another wife to give him sons? Is he going to love her anymore?"

Grandmother stroked my hair. "Your father won't do that. It wasn't her fault the twins died."

Der told me once that when the boys were born, our father was very happy, and he appreciated our mother more. The adults in the village respected Mother more, too.

"What happened to my father's first wife?" I asked.

"She died. Her other children died too."

"Does Toua know?"

Grandmother nodded. "When he was young and immature, he was rude to your mother. He called her stepmother when he didn't get his way. Your mother was angry and hurt because she raised him since he was six months old."

I stared at my hands. "Was my mother married before?"

"Yes, she and her first husband had three sons and three daughters. Her sons died, and her daughters weren't allowed to come with her when she remarried your father."

My mouth fell open and my stomach clenched.

"Your mother lost contact with them," Grandmother continued. "When she had Der, she became an herbalist and studied herbs to cure illnesses so she could help her children."

Where were my other sisters? Were they alive or dead? My mother had ten children, and now only Der and I remained. My poor mother. What did she do to deserve this? I dropped my head into my trembling hands. It was too much for me to bear. A sob racked my body.

Grandmother stroked my hair again. "Take deep breaths.

It's good to cry but don't cry a lot. It'll weaken you. You have to be strong."

"How?" I mumbled.

"Be thankful for your life. Love and cherish what you have now. This is how you stay strong." She paused. "I lost two sons and a daughter to the war, but I'm thankful for my life, and I have your father who keeps me strong."

I took several deep breaths and swiped at my tears with the back of my hands. Mother and Der needed me. I must bring hope to my family.

I steadied my voice. "I know men take care of the parents and keep them safe, but what else?"

"Men help the community clear farmland, build huts, hunt, and many other things that women cannot do. This is why the more sons a woman has, the higher her status in the community. Also, boys carry on the family name."

"Toua is the only son left. I hope nothing happens to him. I want to protect and care for my mother like a boy. Can a girl do that?"

Grandmother hesitated. "It is expected that girls are to get married and take care of their in-laws. For the time being, you can help your mother maintain her status by being a helpful, obedient girl who brings honor to the family." She paused and took a big breath. "If you can make your father proud, he won't regret that you are girl."

I stood and clipped my grandmother's hair to the back of her head with a large, metal barrette. I helped her up from the wooden stool, and she held on to me as we walked slowly to the hut.

Mother sat on the wooden stool just outside the front door crying. I watched her with watery eyes. Grandmother smoothed Mother's hair and entered the home with a hunched back. I sat on the stool with Mother and held her arm and leaned on her shoulder. We both wailed. I cried my heart out for all the misfortunes brought to my family. When we both at last calmed, my heart felt lighter. I took a few deep breaths and was ready to talk.

"Mother, I can't replace the twins, but I can be your boy." I held her arm tighter. "I don't have to marry and move far away. I'll live with you and take good care of you. I promise I'll try my best to do what a boy does."

Mother nodded. She seemed pleased, but I wondered if I'd be able to do what a boy did. Building huts and cutting down trees were difficult tasks. Would I have the ability and strength of a boy? Would people look down on me if I didn't get married? Would I be able to protect my mother from mistreatment?

Father and Toua returned with some wild, edible plants they found around the outskirts of the village. Der wouldn't get up from the cot, leaving me to cook alone, but boiling the plants was easy. If it was cooking rice, I'd worry because my rice never comes out right.

When the food was ready, we all sat together to eat. No one spoke. A quiet chill settled over the hut. Mother's grave face showed she was in a different world. She wouldn't eat. I nudged her, and she looked at the food. It wasn't very tempting, but I picked a plant with my hand and offered it to her. She opened her mouth, and I fed her. It felt good to be helpful.

After we ate, I walked outside. The fallen weeds in the open space reminded me of the night I played with my twin brothers. Thinking about them, anger and grief boiled inside me. The weeds surrounding me seemed like the enemy, and I stomped hard on them, taking my revenge. I smashed every wild plant that stood in my way.

Exhausted, I rested on the ground and looked up at the clear, blue sky. I murmured, "Why wasn't I born a boy? Oh Lord of Heaven, why didn't you make me a boy for my parents?"

My mother had told me stories about how, before babies were born, they lived in the sky, which is heaven. Lord of Heaven sent them to the Earth.

An idea came to me. A way to prove to Mother that I'd keep my word. I remembered that Toua had found a ragged pair of pants in a hut for a change of clothes and had washed and hung them out to dry. I found the pants and put them and Father's knife in my basket. I thought about asking Der for help, but her morning sickness had made her weak and helpless. I hurried to the creek.

Sitting at the edge, I looked at my reflection in the clear water. I smoothed my beautiful waist-length, silky, black strands and parted them evenly on both sides of my face. I was prettier with my hair down and absolutely loved my long hair, but I had to bring hope to my family.

I held a chunk of my hair and cut it off. I sawed through one chunk after another. When I was done, I put on Toua's clothes. I pulled the loose, long black pants up and tucked in the huge black shirt. I fastened my red sash around my waist to secure the pants.

Nearing the home, I found Mother pacing outside the hut. I cleared my throat to sound masculine. "Mother, what are you doing?"

She faced me and shock crossed her face. She had aged a lot in the last few days, with flat cheeks and wrinkles creased around her round eyes and on her forehead.

"What have you done to yourself?" Displeasure laced her voice.

I stopped in front of her with a thin smile. "I know the pain you're going through. Please accept me. I'm your new boy."

She studied me. "Who cut your hair? Girls don't cut their hair that short." She touched my ear-length hair and shook her head. Tears spilled down her cheeks.

My shoulders slumped. I released a breath. "I'm sorry,

Mother. I...I thought you wanted boys. Since the twins are gone, I could be your boy. I...I want to make you happy."

She mustered a smile and stroked my hair. "I know you love me very much and would do anything to make me happy. But I love you for who you are."

I nodded.

"I'm thankful to have two wonderful daughters."

"If you prefer me as a girl, I'll be your daughter," I said. "But I promise, I will stay with you forever to look after you and my father. I don't care if people look down on me for not having a husband."

"You've a kind heart." Pride shone in her eyes. "I'm so lucky you are mine. Please know that you're my life. You're like the sun that saves me in my dream."

"What do you mean?" I asked.

"Your character shows in everything you do like the sunlight that gives living things the energy they need to live. You give me hope, and you're like the sun that shines on me and makes every day brighter."

A fluttering emotion swirled in my belly. Why hadn't she told me this before? Maybe I could be her hope now. Maybe I did exhibit good traits after all but had just been lazy.

"You know what your name means?" she asked.

"The sun," I said.

"Yes. It's a perfect name for you."

"Mother, how did you know to name me Nou?"

"The day before you were born, I had a dream. I was alone and cold in the middle of the woods. The sun came and shone through the trees on and around me and warmed me. It saved my life."

"Why you were in the woods?" I asked. I had never heard this story.

She shook her head. "I don't know why I was in the woods, but when I woke up, I was shaking and sweating. After I had you, I named you Nou because I thought the dream was a message from your ancestors to name you after the sun, the source of all energy."

"Really? So I am like the sun?" I smiled. I was important to my mother even though I was born a girl and never got my chores done right. "I'm sorry for being a laggard. I'll work on it."

"No one is perfect. You hate weeding, but you are my clever daughter. You have potential."

Tears pricked my eyes. Her words gave me new energy. I could be like the sun, bright, hot, and powerful. I never knew that a compliment could lift a person's spirit high with confidence and hope. I'd sacrifice my life for my mother and Der. I could save lives and bring hope to my family like the heroes and heroines who saved their kingdoms in the stories.

Mother took off her blue bandana and put it around my hair. "Don't take it off until your hair grows long again. Now, go put on your own clothes."

I was surprised to find Toua at the door watching. He didn't scold me for wearing his clothes.

"I can take you as a brother," Toua said, sounding serious. "You are capable of helping me."

He was now the only son. He was my parents' hope; the protector and the future who was as valuable as gold.

"I'll help you with anything, especially taking care of our parents," I said.

Toua let out a breath. "I'll let you be their guardian."

I gawked. Was he telling me to take over his duty as a son? Was he overwhelmed or did he simply not care for them? What was a son worth if he was a fool? Toua loved Father, but he had shown no love nor offered any comfort to my mother. If he was her biological son, would he comfort her?

If Toua wanted me to be our parents' guardian, I would. I wouldn't allow my mother to be a burden to anyone.

Chapter Seven

FINALLY, FATHER WAS ABLE TO CONVINCE MOTHER TO ALLOW him and Toua to bury the twins. The men left, leaving Der and me to keep our mother calm in the hut. Father worried Mother would faint seeing the twins being buried. Der sat with Mother on the bamboo cot, stroking her hair. Grandmother and I sat by the fire pit.

A loud knock sounded at the hut door. And a woman called, "Is anybody home?"

Wide-eyed, I looked to Grandmother, Mother, and Der. Where had the woman come from? I hurried to the door and opened it. A petite woman in her late seventies stood outside.

"May I come in?" she said in a weak voice.

I hesitated, then nodded. "Yes, come in."

She entered.

"Hello," Mother said.

"I'm Mrs. Nao Tou. My family lives in the forest," she said.

"Do you mean your family hides in the forest?" I asked.

"My husband and I live there."

"Where are your children?"

Annoyance flitted across her face.

"Enough, Nou," Mother said, then she looked at the woman. "How can we help you?"

"I came here to warn you," the old woman said. "I know what happened to your sons. You need to leave this hut immediately. Other people had children die in this hut. If I had known you were coming, I'd have come sooner to warn you. This hut has evil spirits."

Goose bumps rose on my skin. So the ominous feeling I'd had that first night was correct. The haunted hut and the woman's knowledge of the twins' death chilled me. There was no one around when the boys died. How could the woman know? I wished she could have come earlier.

Mother's shoulders slumped and her lips trembled. Tears leaked from her tired eyes. Mrs. Nao Tou apologized and told us she had to return to her home before dark. As soon as she left, we gathered our belongings and rushed outside to the trampled weeds. Grandmother and I sat on the weeds. Mother didn't seem to know what to do, and she wandered off. Der followed her.

"Grandmother, do you believe this hut has evil spirits?" I said in a shaky voice.

"Yes. Spirits are everywhere, good and evil. Without a permanent home, our house spirits are wandering and not protecting the family."

"Do bad spirits follow people around trying to hurt them?"

"No, but if people step on their boundaries and offend them, then they will retaliate and bring illness," Grandmother replied.

I hazarded a glance at the hut. "So we invaded the evil spirits in the hut?"

Grandmother tucked strands of white hair behind her ears and nodded. "If there had been a shaman to tell the evil spirits that we were sorry we didn't know they were in the hut first, the twins would have been saved."

The black crow suddenly rose in memory. Had the crow brought us a bad omen? Or was it a good bird to warn me of the tragedies coming my way like the old woman warning us of the hut?

"Grandmother, before the attack while I was weeding in the field, a black crow flew to me and landed on my shoulder. Why do you think it landed on me?" I asked.

"Did you tell your parents?"

"No."

"If you'd told them, they'd have done something about it."

"The attack happened right after, so they couldn't have done anything," I replied. Was I correct, or had my silence brought bad luck to my family?

Silence descended.

"I think the crow was warning you of the danger and telling you to be careful." Grandmother coughed. "Don't think about it and let it bother you."

I nodded but wasn't sure I could forget about the crow.

As Toua and Father returned, Der and Mother arrived.

Mother told Father about the old woman and their conversation.

"We need to leave immediately," said Father.

"I can't leave my boys." Mother's voice cracked.

"I'm sorry." Father blinked away tears. "We can't stay here."

"You all go. I'm going to stay here with my boys."

"We're going together," said Father firmly.

"We must go." I pulled my mother's arm. "Please."

Mother looked at me, then slowly nodded. It seemed I was her hope. My chest felt lighter.

As we entered the woods and the wind soughed through the trees, I shivered with cold. An image of the old woman flashed in my head. How did she know we were there and the twins had died? Was she a human or a ghost? Maybe she heard the family's loud cries. I was thankful she told us to leave. Otherwise, Der and I could be next.

No one spoke. No birds chirped. Mother frequently glanced over her shoulder toward the place where her beloved sons were buried. It pained me to watch. First, I pulled Der, and now my mother. I was traumatized, too, but I needed to be strong for them both. I wished I had magic power so that I could give them hope.

By late afternoon, Grandmother's pace slowed until she hardly moved. We halted and Father squatted for her to get on his back. Mother watched them and wept.

I squatted for my mother. "I'll carry you like Father carries his mother."

Mother shook her head.

"I can carry you," I insisted. "I'm almost as tall as you."

"You'd break your bones." Toua turned to me. "You're fragile like a shell. Don't dare challenge yourself."

I was not physically strong yet, but I would grow stronger. I'd prove myself to them.

"He's right." Mother swiped at her tears with the back of her hands. "I can walk. My feet are fine."

Mother might be fine physically but not mentally. Why didn't Toua offer help or comfort? She raised him since he was six months old. I started to believe the stories I heard about stepsons neglecting their elderly stepmoms. I hoped Toua would change.

"Mother, when I'm older, I'm going to build a huge hut and care for you and any elders who have no son or no home," I said. "I'm going to take care of the unfortunate."

"That's very sweet of you." Mother gave a faint smile. "Do you know that it might not be possible? It's not a paying job. It would be hard to find volunteers to help you and tend to your elderly people when they have to work to feed themselves."

"When we win the war and I can read and we live in the huge hut, I'll read stories to you," I said.

Mother nodded, eyes glistening with tears. She cried as easily as a baby. Why didn't Father cry as much? Maybe that was how men showed their courage. As a soldier once, Father had learned to cope.

Grandmother was fortunate she had a family that cared for her. Without us, she'd be a burden to someone else, and they would leave her behind for sure. Mother and Der needed me as much as Grandmother needed the family. I had a tough job ahead, and I must do everything in my power to support them.

Chapter Eight

Within a month, my family traveled through Pha Te and Sa Xia villages. Instability and the unsuccessful search for Pheng wore on us. Many refugees flocked to the new village, Pha Khao, so we followed them in hope of finding a safer life.

Pha Khao, like many villages, was located in a carved valley surrounded by densely-forested mountains that stretched into the distance. New huts were scattered throughout, clusters of stout brown blocks that spread over the valley.

Gia Xa Lee was the Nai Ban, the village leader. He assigned Nao Bee Vang to house my family. Nao Bee was in his late thirties and had four young children. He shared the same Vang clan and called me sister.

More families moved in from the nearby villages. To accommodate the newcomers, Gia Xa asked the villagers to help build more thatch huts. The men and women who volunteered to help build our home came to assist. The men cut wood to frame the hut and split bamboo for the walls, while the women gathered long elephant grasses and weaved them for the roof.

Usually, I didn't care for such tasks, but this time I wanted to learn. I asked Nao Bee to allow me to build the hut with them and was denied. As a girl, I was assigned to babysit his daughters, ages three and five, because that's what girls do. In the adults' eyes, girls were physically incapable. They were given the easiest jobs. Nao Bee's boys were younger than me but got to trim tree branches with the men.

I wanted to bring honor to my family and earn respect from the community, so I followed orders and worked hard. While I cared for the girls, I watched the builders and helped them whenever I could. Sometimes I carried the three-year-old on my back with the baby carrier and brought water to the builders. When the girls took their naps, I brought elephant grasses for the women and picked up debris afterward. Der worked hard, as well. She weaved grasses with the women, and she cooked for the people.

The simple rectangular home was done within six days. It was a big room with three bamboo cots on one side, a fire pit, mud stove and dining area on the other side. Our home was on a hillside, six huts from Nao Bee.

Food was scarce. Like most villagers, my family cleared small plots to grow food, but there were no seeds to plant. Only weeds grew on the bare land. Starvation seemed to be imminent and foraging for edible plants in the woods became a routine for Der and me.

One evening I overheard Father and Gia Xa talking quietly in the backyard. Gia Xa explained that he sent a message to the United States Agency for International Development (USAID), a program for war victims. He requested food, seeds, and livestock for the villagers. Gia Xa and many refugees received food from the program prior to the cease-fire agreement in 1973. After the cease-fire agreement, the refugees no longer received food and were forced to move to Pha Khao. Gia Xa hoped USAID would respond to his request.

. . .

A WEEK LATER, I RETURNED HOME FROM THE WOODS AND unloaded my basket of firewood. After gulping a mouthful of water from the green plastic canteen, I rested on my cot. A thundering sound reverberated, and I jumped to my feet.

The people shouted, "An airplane! An airplane!"

My father rushed outside, with the family close behind. We looked up at the enormous machine in the clear, blue sky.

"It's a helicopter," said Father. "It looks like it will land next to Gia Xa's hut. I'm going to see who it is."

"I'm coming with you." I ran after him.

Gia Xa's hut was on the west side of the valley, and northwest of his hut was a small clearing.

When we reached Gia Xa's home, the helicopter, a dark green thing with spinning wings and a long tail, had landed on the field. The helicopter sounded like waves of thunder, and gusts of wind from the helicopter's blades bent the tall weeds. I had never seen such a marvel.

Like us, some of the villagers gathered near the helicopter to see who had arrived. A moment later, a man emerged from inside.

The people shouted, "Than Pop! Than Pop!"

He approached us. Some people pushed themselves free of the crowd to shake hands with him. I gazed in awe. There he stood, the man I had heard about and had always wished to meet! Edgar Buell had given Father the two Laotian books that were burned in our hut. Than Pop was his code name, and he had supervised schools for children in Long Chieng and Sam Thong and supplied them with books. At Long Chieng, Father met Edgar while he was a soldier, and Father learned to read and write in Hmong.

"Father, your American friend is here," I said. "I'm going to ask him for books."

Father smiled.

The people crowded around Than Pop like honeybees in a

swarm. Gia Xa shouted at the villagers to stand in line so everyone would have a chance to greet him. They made two long lines of about thirty people along the dirt path. Than Pop greeted each person, including the children.

I waited patiently at the end of the line. Than Pop was taller than the Hmong men in the crowd, and he was nearly bald with some gray streaks mixed with what little dark hair that remained on his head. His eyeglasses rested on his high, big nose and covered his deep, blue eyes. Though he spent time out in the sun teaching farmers how to grow food, he was still white compared to the villagers.

I was equally excited and nervous. Being poor and uneducated, I felt so small, so low in status to shake hands with such an important person from America. Why would Than Pop shake hands with unimportant people? I had heard that leaders and famous people only shook the hands of people who shared their status. My turn finally came. I let out a breath and shyly lifted my right hand.

Than Pop said, "Hello" in Hmong.

Astonished, I said, "Hello. You can speak...Hmong?"

"Yes, but not fluently."

He released my hand. I smiled, feeling like I was flying after shaking hands with this famous American.

Than Pop shook hands with Father and said, "Old friend, good to see you again."

"It's an honor to meet you again," said Father.

I quickly interrupted, "Than Pop, you gave my father two books, and he gave them to me, but the Communists burned them. Do you have any more?"

"I'm sorry. I don't have any more literature books," he replied, his accent heavy. "But I have a novel I'm reading and it's in the helicopter. I can give you that one."

"Yes!" I shouted, then averted my eyes in respect.

"It's written in English," he said.

I looked up. “English? I can’t even read Hmong or Lao”

He smiled. “That’s okay, you will learn to read English.”

I sighed happily. “Thank you. I’ll take it, and hopefully I’ll learn to read.”

“I’ll give it to you before I leave.”

“I know you’re in a hurry, but I’ve one quick question.” Words spilled out of my mouth as fast as the wind because I worried he would run from me.

He waited patiently.

“I heard the United States is a powerful country. I’m sure the Americans can win if they choose to. Can you please ask your people to come back to finish the war? Don’t let us die. Our lives are like this because we got involved in the fighting.”

His eyes widened. “Such a clever girl. What’s your name?”

I straightened. “Nou Vang. I know you care about us.”

“Nou, if I didn’t love your people, I wouldn’t be here. I’ll always remember you. You’re right that America is a powerful country. We can’t always do what we want, but I’ll do what I can to help the Hmong.”

I smiled in relief. “Thank you.” I couldn’t believe he listened and talked with me, a girl. I felt important, honored, and lucky.

The crowd followed him to Gia Xa’s hut. The home was too small to fit everyone, so Than Pop decided to talk to the villagers outside the home.

“Hello, my fellow Hmong,” he said in a loud voice. “I’m happy to see you all today. I came back from Thailand yesterday to see you for the last time and heard that many of you moved here and needed help. I’ll do what I can to help you.”

“Than Pop,” Father called. “Our lives are unstable, and our future is uncertain. For the time being we need seeds to plant and livestock to raise. We also need food until our crops are ready to harvest.”

Than Pop nodded. “I’ll call the CIA advisors in Thailand

about your situation before I leave. If I don't get a response from them, I will let them know as soon as I get to Thailand. Thank you for allowing me to work with you all these years. You're a great people, and I thank you for teaching me your culture and language. I will miss you."

"We will miss you, too," said Father. "Thank you for everything you've done for us. You're a great man. Some of us can read because of you."

Gia Xa led Than Pop and the group on the dirt path on a tour of the village. Except for a few huts that needed roofing and framing, the new huts were finished. The group stopped at the edge of the village and Than Pop stared out at bare fields that stretched from valley to hill. Without seed, the people couldn't grow food. They began walking back toward the helicopter.

When the helicopter came into sight up ahead, it's propellor turning, Than Pop stopped and faced the villagers who watched him with hollow eyes and sunken cheeks. "I will help," Than Pop said, then again walking toward the helicopter. "Goodbye, my friends."

"Are we going to see you again?" a few people asked, as they walked with him.

"I'm sure we'll meet again."

"I want the book you promised me!" I shouted over the roar of the helicopter.

Than Pop grinned and beckoned me closer. I pushed past Father and hurried after Than Pop as he ducked inside the helicopter. Father reached me and grabbed my arm before I reached the helicopter. The noise of the machine hurt my ears and the wind whipped my hair around my face. Than Pop emerged from the helicopter with a book and hurried to us. He led us far enough away from the helicopter that he could speak without shouting.

Than Pop handed me the book. "Nou, it hurts me to see a

curious child like you with no opportunity for school. You are the first child to ask me for books. Other children ask for money. I wish you could come to America. There, you could attend school all day."

"All day?" I shouted. "I'd love that! How do I get to America?"

Than Pop looked at Father and said, "Your daughter is unique. I can take her to America for a better life if you give me permission."

"A few Hmong officials sent their children to America for education, but they have money. I don't," Father said sadly.

"I'll take care of her," Than Pop said.

Father's eyes lit. "Thank you. Very generous of you." He turned to me, his expression serious. "Your mother is not here, but this is your opportunity. You'll have a better life in America."

Better life and school? My chest burst with happiness. My dreams were coming true! I had luck after all. I couldn't stop smiling. Then, my smile faded as I realized that I would be forced to leave my family behind.

My heart raced. "Do I leave now?"

"Yes," Than Pop said. "I can't remain here. It's not safe for the pilot or me."

Oh Heaven! This was my opportunity, the best that life offered. But what about Mother and Der? Could I break my promise and go to a country far, far away?

"Than Pop, if I go with you, will I see my family again?"

"I hope so, but I can't guarantee you will."

I bit my lip. Education or family? Would Der and Mother want me to go? Would they be happy or sad? I drew in a deep breath. I couldn't break my promises to them. I loved stories and wanted a better life, but guilt would torture and kill me if I didn't fulfill my promises.

"Thank you, Than Pop, for offering me the opportunity. I can't leave my family." Tears pricked my eyes.

"I understand." He handed the book to me. "Good luck."

Father asked Than Pop, "How long is the USAID crew staying in Laos?"

"I think they are leaving this month," Than Pop replied. "Captain Fred Walker, chief pilot of Air America, will probably be the last one to leave."

The pilot called for Than Pop, and he boarded the plane. I didn't have a chance to ask him what the book was about, or even the title.

Father and I joined the crowd. The helicopter lifted off the ground, and it flew higher and higher. How could humans make such a powerful thing? What did one need to make it? We watched the helicopter until it disappeared in the far west.

"Father, why can't we make helicopters to take us around?" I asked.

"Money and education. Our country is poor. If we are not at war, then some children will be able to go to school."

Children like me. I was anxious to show Der my new book and ran home.

At the door, I stopped to catch my breath. "Der, look what I've got!" I hurried to the guest bamboo cot where she lay and showed her the book.

Der smiled wanly. "I'm happy for you."

I sat on the edge of the bed and opened the book. I turned page by page. It was a thick book with many headings. What stories lived on these pages?

"I hope there is a love story," said Der.

"I hope so, too. When I can read, I'll read it to you." I breathed deeply. "Than Pop offered to take me to America to study."

Der bolted upright. "No. You can't leave us!"

"Why not?"

"I need you." Tears shimmered in her eyes.

As my sister and second mother, I always needed her. But in my mind, I was a burden because I relied on her for everything. I was a useless girl in everyone's eyes. Now I was needed.

"That's why I didn't leave," I said.

Her face relaxed. "Thank you. You are the best sister in the world. You should know that having you to talk to has kept me alive. Without you, I would have died of sadness and depression."

"I'd never leave you and Mother," I promised.

Der's smile made staying worthwhile.

TWO WEEKS LATER, AN AIRPLANE FLEW OVER THE VILLAGE AND dropped sacks of rice, corn and vegetable seeds. Later that same day, another airplane dropped off cages with parachutes. The villagers found about one hundred chickens and fifty piglets in the cages, and they brought the livestock to Gia Xa's hut. He distributed the bags of seeds and rice among the people equally. Since the livestock couldn't be divided equally, some families ended up with either two piglets, a male and a female to raise, or two chickens. My family got a hen and a rooster. Any resulting chicks would be given to other families who were in need.

This time I got to build a chicken coop with Father and Toua. I was proud of myself. Slowly, I was learning the skills I needed to be the daughter I wanted to be. Every day I foraged around the woods for insects and worms to feed the chickens.

I started a garden south of our hut and planted the gai choy seeds, green onions, chili peppers, and cilantro. To prevent the villagers' chickens from eating my vegetables, I fenced my garden with bamboo strips in a rectangular plot. I tended my garden most evenings after I came home from the fields.

My parents cleared more land to grow opium poppies in October. With people moving in, we had to claim land before it was taken. Opium poppy was the only cash crop, so every family grew it. I hoped for stability in the village, so we could harvest opium and trade it for goods. The family needed new clothes and shoes. While we tended the rice field, an airplane flew low over our heads.

Father looked up. "No airplane has come so close to the village like this. I think it is Captain Fred Walker stopping by to say goodbye to the villagers."

Gazing at the clear, blue sky, I murmured, "All the Americans are gone."

"Not all. Jerry 'Hog' Daniels is still with General Vang Pao in Long Chieng."

Hope tightened my chest. "That means we're not losing the war yet. But how can we win without the Americans?"

Father ignored my question and went back to work.

After that, Father slept even less than before. All the Americans leaving Laos concerned the villagers. The men gathered at Gia Xa's home every day. Father was hardly home, and his dull eyes told me he was afraid. The Communists would not be merciful toward any former CIA soldiers.

Chapter Nine

THE BLUE CLOUDS BLOCKED THE SUN FOR THE MOMENT, COOLING Der and me a little as we finished washing clothes at the stream. We put the clothes in our bamboo baskets and shared a seat on a rock. I leaned on Der's shoulder with my eyes closed and my feet in the knee-high water. The rustling of leaves and murmuring sound of the flowing water soothed my anxiety.

"Nou!" a man shouted.

Startled, I jerked around to see who had called my name. Blong Thao, a neighbor's son, and his friend walked down the trail toward us. The men each had a bow and arrow in their hands and carried dark green backpacks.

"You scared us. What are you doing here?" I asked.

"Sorry." Blong half-smiled. "We came from hunting."

The men reached the stream and stood on the edge. Blong clamped a hand on the other man's shoulder.

"This is my friend, Neng Moua."

"Nice meeting you, Nou and Der." Neng, short and tan, mustered a smile.

"Did Blong tell you our names?" I asked.

“Yes.” Neng inched closer to Der. “I heard that your husband is missing. Do you have any news of his situation?”

Der shook her head. With her belly showing, everyone was talking about her. Der’s beauty put her in the public eye, and the news spread like wildfire.

“I’m sorry. Why aren’t you with his family?” he asked.

“His family escaped while she was visiting us.” It was a good lie, and I had practiced it, so it slipped out easily.

Neng sighed. “It’s hard to believe that your husband left his beautiful wife and didn’t bother to look for her.”

Der lowered her head.

A flush of heat rose to my cheeks. “Enough of your talk. Please leave us alone.”

“If your husband is dead, I’d love to take care of you and your child,” Neng said, as they turned to leave.

“In your dreams!” I yelled.

The men hurried away.

Tears slid down Der’s cheeks. I stroked her hair.

“Nou, you want to protect me, but you are ruining your reputation.” She sniffled. “You’ve become a mean girl. Don’t yell at people. Let them say all they want.”

“No. I won’t allow that.” I released a breath. “Der, you can’t let mean people put you down. If you hear them repeating rumors, tell them to stop.”

“It’s easy to say.”

“Have some courage and yell at them. It might stop them.”

“When you’re in my shoes, you have no courage,” she said in a flat voice. “You don’t know what I’m going through. If I didn’t believe Pheng is alive, I’d have committed suicide.”

I knew the shame she was living with. I squeezed her hand. “I love you, Der. Promise me you won’t harm yourself or the baby.”

She squeezed my hand back. “I promise you. I’ll find Pheng, get married and live happily forever.”

Since the pregnancy, Der had changed. She felt her pregnancy degraded Father, a well-respected man in the community. Father no longer bragged to his friends about his beautiful, hardworking, and reliable daughter.

To protect Der from more insults, I tried to keep her away from people. When at home, Der did all the cooking while I washed clothes, carried water, gathered food, and tended to the livestock. Out in the field, Der had more freedom. Every family was busy on their farm and had no time to gossip.

A few nights later before bedtime, my parents came over to our cot.

"Der," Mother said, "Wa Leng Moua and his son approached your father and me this evening. His son likes you and wants to know if he can marry you. I lied a few times to cover for you, but people suspect you don't have a husband. I want you to know that I told Wa Leng you are available to get married. They are coming to ask for your marriage tomorrow."

Der shook her head.

"What is his son's name?" I asked.

"Neng Moua," Father said.

That ugly, short man who insulted Der at the stream!

"He likes you and doesn't mind that you are pregnant," Father said. "If you marry him, the rumors about you will stop, and you will have a home to have your baby. He'll take care of you and your child."

"Father, I don't want to marry anyone other than Pheng. How can I marry someone I don't love?" She half sobbed. "I'd rather be miserable without a husband than marry someone I don't like. I hope you understand."

Father exchanged a look with mother, then said, "Der, we don't know if Pheng is alive. I want you to marry Neng. This man loves you and wants to protect you and your child. You will learn to love him."

"No," Der cried. "I can't marry him. Please don't allow them to come tomorrow. I won't be home."

"I want you to have a life and your child to have a father." Father raised his voice.

"I can't do it. I'm sorry," Der said in a high-pitched voice.

Father shook his head. Der had never refused anything our parents had asked of her before. Father's obedient daughter had turned into a defiant one.

I agreed with Father. It seemed like the best solution, but I had to support my sister. Three against one would only make things worse for Der.

"Father, if she doesn't want to marry Neng, please don't force her."

Mother looked from Father to Der. "Der, you might regret it later," she said. "Know that you can't give birth in our home. We'll have to find a place for you, and you must stay there for a month. Will you be all right with that?"

Father explained that only children of the family's clan could be born in the home and accepted by the ancestral spirits. If the family angered the spirits, misfortune could come to the family. Though Der was a Vang clan, her child was not. She either accepted the marriage or followed the strict tradition.

"I understand the hardship ahead." Der's voice was thick with emotion. "I've made my decision. I have a feeling Pheng is alive, and I'll wait for him."

"All right," said Father, "if that's what you choose. Please know that I only want the best for you. Your mother and I don't want to see you suffer."

"I know," she said in a small voice.

I always wanted to support Der, but what if Pheng was dead?

Chapter Ten

December brought cold winds, but we had some new hope. One of the poppy fields was ready to harvest, and Der's belly was as round as a pumpkin. A child added to the family and opium to trade for new clothes gave my spirits a lift.

Each day, I worked hard to incise the poppy seedpods with my multi-bladed tool. Each milky drop from the seedpod was money, so adrenaline rushed through me as I worked. I didn't take breaks and tried to keep up with my parents and brother. Stories and education faded from my mind as concern for Der and Grandmother took precedence. Grandmother needed care, and Der was due any day.

In the afternoon, the family took time off from harvesting to gather elephant grasses and bamboo poles. With the materials, I helped Father and Toua build a lean-to, a small space attached to the thatch hut, for Der to have her baby. The lean-to was big enough for three people to sleep. It had a fire pit to keep the infant warm.

After the first week of harvesting, Father traveled to a city in the lowland and traded opium for polyester fleece blankets, sandals, green and red sashes, and black fabric. Mother started sewing black pants and shirts for everyone.

One morning, Der's water broke, and Mother and I stayed home with her. It was close to noon when her contractions began. She put on Pheng's ring to give her strength. Mother and I took her to the lean-to, and she lay on the dried elephant grasses. While Mother coached Der, I started the fire.

As her labor progressed, Der screamed. Mother sent me on tasks. Typically, when a woman gave birth, a couple of experienced women would be called to help, but since Der's child was out of wedlock, Mother tried to keep it as private as possible.

I made two trips to the stream for water. Next, I had to kill a chicken to cook for Der, which I didn't know how to do because Der had always done the killing and most of the cooking. I caught one in the coop easily, but there was no one to assist me with the hard part. I breathed deeply and understood why my mother wanted me to learn everything. My father and brother arrived then. Father prayed at the altar for Der, and Toua sat by the fire pit.

"Toua, can you help me kill this chicken?" I asked.

"You don't know how?" He laughed softly.

"It needs two people, one holding the chicken and one killing it."

"It's a small chicken. You can do it yourself."

"If I could do it, I wouldn't ask you," I snapped.

Toua shook his head. "You are not ready to get married. You won't be able to serve your husband and in-laws."

I scowled. "Who says I'm getting married soon?"

"Hard working girls marry between ages sixteen and eighteen. I don't see that you'd be ready by then."

I didn't want to argue, but Toua was getting under my skin. "I don't care, and I don't want to get married at that age. What about you? You are eighteen and not married. Something's wrong with you."

"Stop immediately," Father scolded. "Toua, go help Nou, now!"

Toua jumped to his feet. We killed the chicken, and I cooked it. But I still had more chores, dinner to finish and livestock to tend. Without Der and Mother's help, I felt the weight of their chores. Despite the cold, beads of sweat formed on my forehead. One good thing, all the work kept me from thinking about Der's pain.

"It's a boy!" Mother finally shouted from the lean-to.

I stopped sweeping and laughed heartily. "Yes, a son! Thank you, Lord of Heaven!" Energy filled me and I ran with Father and Toua to the lean-to.

Mother smiled, holding the beautiful baby in her arms. Father took the infant from her. As he looked at the child, his lips stretched wide into the biggest smile ever. My exhaustion disappeared. Even Der managed to grin through her pain. It was a moment of joy and hope. Toua held the baby after Father. Everyone seemed to forgive Der for shaming the family. Even without a husband, a son raised Der's status.

Der groaned, holding her stomach.

I yelped, "Mother, what's wrong?"

"Stomach cramps happen after birth. It'll go away." Mother massaged Der's stomach.

Late that night, in the lean-to with Der, Mother yawned frequently. Finally, her head fell forward.

"Mother, you go sleep," I whispered. "I've got Der and the baby."

Mother's head jerked up. "I'm fine."

"Go to sleep," I insisted.

"All right. Call if you need help."

After she left, I put more wood in the fire and lay on the dried grasses next to the newborn. He was adorable. His cheeks were as soft as the blanket and his lips were red like tomatoes. Der bent her legs and grimaced, holding her stomach. I wanted to help her, but my body was too heavy to move.

A while later, Der groaned in pain, again. Slowly, I sat up because I had no choice. I moved over and massaged Der's stomach. Her stomach cramps kept us up all night. Occasionally I'd put more wood in the fire to keep us warm. Barking dogs gave me goose bumps. We were vulnerable to strangers, animals, or ghosts. I wanted to be inside the home with my parents, grandmother, and brother. A month in the lean-to would be a long time.

At dawn, the infant cried. Der breastfed him. Later, he wailed again. I held him tight to keep him warm. My eyes grew heavy, and my stomach growled. I barely had energy to move, but daylight approached. I had to cook breakfast for Der, wash clothes, and tend to other chores. I jerked awake, realizing I'd moaned out loud.

"I'm sorry you haven't slept all night," said Der softly.

My eyes fully opened. "It's all right. I'm just tired. I can do this."

"It's hard work to care for me and my child." Her voice cracked with emotion.

"You raised me since I was five. I'm happy to help you."

"I appreciate your help. Thank you."

I would cook three meals, rice and chicken boiled with herbs, for Der each day. This would be her diet for a month. Culture dictated that on the third day, the family would have a soul-calling ceremony to welcome the newborn. He would receive his name and many blessing strings tied to his hands from the community.

On the third morning, Father asked Der to give her child a name. She named him Nhia, meaning silver. That was it. No soul calling. No celebration. My parents had tears in their eyes, for they loved the child, but there was nothing they could do for a child born out of wedlock. They left for the field.

Der wept, making tears burn behind my eyes. She'd cried many times throughout her pregnancy because she missed Pheng and hated the rumors and the shame. But today she cried for her son. The poor child didn't deserve this shame.

I was helpless. "I'm sorry, Der."

Der howled, and Nhia fussed.

I took the child. "We'll find Pheng, and he will have a big celebration for Nhia to claim him as a Yang clan."

I wasn't optimistic about finding him, but I didn't know what else to say. I didn't like Neng Moua, but if Der had married him, he'd have done a soul calling for Nhia. He would've claimed him as a Moua clan, and I wouldn't have to work so hard. Sometimes I growled Pheng's name out of frustration. For now, though, I stayed quiet.

I disliked being the middle child, but now as I reflected on my position in the family, I decided being in the middle was good. I gained knowledge from watching my older and younger siblings. From my mother I learned that if I gave birth to boys, I wouldn't spoil them and treat them as if they were superior to my daughters. Der's situation gave me insight into the complexity of life. Actions and choices had consequences. From my brother, I had learned to kill a chicken. Even my cooking had improved. These days, my mother gave me more compliments than scolding. That had to be a good thing.

Chapter Eleven

MAY 1975

LATELY, A FEW FAMILIES HAD STOPPED TENDING THEIR FIELDS. Evening conversations among the neighbors stopped. Each family whispered quietly to themselves. The strangeness made me anxious and restless. One afternoon, when Father and Toua went to Gia Xa's home, I tagged along to find out what was happening. The home was empty, and the livestock wandered everywhere.

"What happened?" I asked, panic raising.

"We lost the war," said Father.

My stomach twisted into a knot.

"Why did they flee without telling us?" My voice was shrill with anger and terror.

"Soften your voice." Fear crossed Toua's face.

I blew out a frustrated breath. I had learned to whisper a year ago, but I couldn't help it when I became distraught. A year had gone by, and I was now fourteen.

Father's expression darkened with worry. "They can't tell us because the leaders must flee first. Their lives are in danger. Gia Xa must have left yesterday morning."

"But your life is in danger, too," I said.

Father remained quiet. I hated the secrets. I hated how people were treated based on their status. Now that we lost the war, everyone's life mattered, not just the officials.

On our way home, we ran into Nao Bee.

"Good morning, Uncle Wa Shoua. I was looking for you." Nao Bee glanced around for people who might be nearby. "Should we go talk at your home?"

"Right here will be fine," Father whispered. "Gia Xa's family is gone."

"They fled to Thailand yesterday. Jerry Daniels, General Vang Pao, and all the military leaders are gone," said Nao Bee. "We must flee. Five other families and I are planning to leave tomorrow morning. Your family can join us. We'll have about two weeks of walking through the jungles—as long as we encounter no danger."

Two weeks? I shivered.

"That's too long," said Father. "My mother won't survive the trip. We should go to Vientiane and hire merchants to help us cross to Thailand."

He shook his head. "That's not an option now. You can't get through without a pass. Meet me at my hut tonight if you decide to leave with us. Keep this information confidential." Nao Bee hurried away.

Fear pulsated inside me, closing on my throat. Heaven, what would happen to us?

"Father, we must follow the General," said Toua, his voice edged with fear. "You're a former CIA soldier. The Communists will arrest you if we stay."

Father shook his head. "I'm worried about your grandmother. Traveling is risky for her."

Once we reached home, Father gathered everyone around him. "We lost the war and Thailand seems to be our best choice. Mother, I'd like to know how you feel about going."

Fear and sadness flashed across her features. She lowered her head. "Heaven, I'm too old for the journey. I don't know how much longer I will live. I'm afraid to go to a foreign country. It might be worse there than here." Tears shimmered in her eyes. "My wish is to die in my country, but if your life is in danger, I have no choice. I don't want you to suffer carrying me and to risk your life for me anymore."

My mother smoothed Grandmother's hair. "The journey would not be safe for you and the baby. I think we'll be all right staying here for a while."

"Yes, I think we'll be fine." Father's soft words belied his stricken look.

Nhia was asleep on Der's right arm, and I kissed him on the cheek. I reached for my sister's left arm. We locked arms.

"What do you think, Der? Stay or leave?" I asked.

"If Father thinks it's better to go, I'd say we go, but I'm worried about my baby and Grandmother."

"Me too," I said, but I feared we wouldn't be safe staying.

Every day Father tried to get news from any messengers who passed by. Fear had stolen his concentration and sleep. General Vang Pao's exile and the Communists' retaliation had caused the exodus. Half the villagers had fled, leaving those of us who remained vulnerable.

When Father and Toua went to the outskirts of the village to see a messenger, I tagged along. In the woods, a man in his thirties sat on a log before twenty men who sat on the ground around and in between the trees. I was the only girl there. The men stared at me.

One man glared at Father. "This meeting is only for men."

Another man, eyes narrowed, asked Father in a harsh voice

that made me feel queasy, "What is she doing here? She should be doing chores like a proper young Hmong girl."

Anger bubbled in my gut. I squeezed my lips tight to suppress hurtful words from escaping my mouth. My father narrowed his eyes on the man. The air turned cold and tense. Everyone waited for Father to speak.

Finally, in a hard voice, Father said, "My daughter is curious. She is brave enough to know the truth. There is no reason to stop someone, not even a girl, from learning. I'm confident that everything we discuss here will be kept confidential."

I loved my father. He was an educated man and valued girls, and he gave me many opportunities. I didn't care if the other men thought I was not being a proper girl or too young to know the facts. I had the right to find out what the future held for us.

Two more men arrived.

"I think that's everybody." Shoua Neng Vang, Father's relative, spoke to the man sitting on the log.

"I'm Koua Xiong," said the man. "My commander, Cher Pao Vang, sent me here to share some news with you. The Pathet Lao arrested Blong, one of our troops, and sent him to a seminar camp. They forced him into intense labor from dawn to dusk. Some captives were put in holes in the ground with no food. The Pathet Lao have killed commanders and anyone who they suspected had the American brain. Blong managed to escape the camp."

A shiver of cold spread through me. I drew in a deep breath.

A man asked, "How do the Pathet Lao know who has the American brain?"

"CIA soldiers. Anyone who speaks some English," said Koua. "Believe it or not, if you have a gift or something from America, you are said to have the American brain. The enemy wants to get rid of everyone who was influenced by the Americans."

I gasped, and my heart fluttered wildly. The book Than Pop gave me was in English. If I was caught with the book, I'd be dead. So would Father, who had the list of American names. Father's eyes remained downcast. Being a former CIA soldier, he had every reason to be fearful.

"The Pathet Lao are searching everywhere for former soldiers," said Koua. "If you are one, you need to flee to the jungle before they find you. The resistance fighters will assist you there. I don't know when the enemy will be here but take precautions."

I despised the thought of living in the jungle, but my family had no choice.

On the way home, I asked, "Father, is there any place for us other than the jungle?"

He hesitated. "We have no place to go other than to join the resistance fighters and their families in the forests."

As soon as we got home, I went to my bed and took out the book under the blanket I used as pillow. I sat on the bed, felt the book's cover and studied the prints. Where could I hide it? Toua was nearby and peeked in. He snatched the book from me and turned the pages.

"Give it back!" I shouted.

"I believe this book is English," he snapped. "The person who gave you this wants our family killed."

"That's not true! I asked for it!"

He stared at me. "Then I better destroy it before the Communists get here."

"No! You can't do that!"

His face flushed red in anger. "Do you want our family to get killed?"

I slumped. "Of course not."

"Then burn it."

"Give it back. I'll do it myself," I promised.

Toua hesitated, then handed me the book. I hated everything he said, but he was right.

That evening I made a fire near my garden. Alone, I hugged the book close. The book was all that remained of my dream. Tears blurred my vison. Than Pop's book was invaluable, but I couldn't risk my family getting caught with an American book. My blood boiled as I cursed the war for destroying my hopes, dreams, and future.

Losing the war was like losing my eyes. I now lived in a life of darkness where I would never find my way to freedom. Whichever way I turned, I was going to bump into something that would kill me. There was no clear future for me or my family.

I must have cried for a long while because when I wiped my eyes clear, some pages were damp. I kissed the book and turned the pages over many times.

I took a deep breath and said, "I'm sorry, Than Pop. I have no choice."

I ripped off the first page, lit it on fire, and murmured, "This page is for the education that I didn't get." I tore the second page and lit it. "This is for all the sad stories that I won't get to read and shed tears." The third page. "This is for all the funny stories that I won't get to laugh over." Page four. "This is for the Americans who created this mess and ran home when they knew they couldn't win." Page five. "This is for our miserable life."

My heart burst in pain. Burning the book, the one thing I treasured the most, felt like burning myself.

Der came out and found me. "Why are you burning your book? Isn't it your dream?"

"My dream is dead," I said coldly. "No point in keeping the book."

"I'm sorry." Der slipped an arm around my shoulder.

Mother rushed over with Nhia pressed close to her chest. "Nou, are you all right?"

"She's burning her book," Der said with sadness.

"Please don't let this chaos destroy your hopes, dreams, and courage," Mother said. "Remember, your father told us to not allow our misery to ruin our self-esteem and kill us."

I wanted to tell Mother and Der the reason for burning the book but didn't want them to further pity me or be more afraid. "I don't need it anymore. It won't help me with my life."

Mother said, "I told you that stories won't help you with your life, but if the book gives you hope, you should keep it."

I threw the rest of the book in the fire. "It's better not to have it."

After supper, everyone sat quietly around the fire pit as Father spoke. "At dawn tomorrow, we are going to join the resistance fighters in the forest. I've weighed the options, and this is the better choice. It will not be easy, but it'll save our lives."

"Father, I'm worried about Nhia and Grandmother's safety in the jungle," Der said. "Can the women stay?"

He shook his head. "That's not an option now. The Communists torture and kill the women and children to get to the men." Father paused, then said in a shaky voice, "A source told me that yesterday morning the Pathet Lao arrested a former soldier and his family and took them to the forest. The villagers heard gunshots."

I held my breath and clutched my hands to my chest.

"The hiding is temporary—just until things calm down," said Father. "Pack everything you can. We leave before the villagers get up."

Der turned frightened eyes on me. I wanted to assure her but couldn't find the words. The prospect of the Pathet Lao arresting us was one thing. The danger in the jungle was another.

"Life can't be harder than this. Can it?" A few tears slid down Grandmother's wrinkled, pale cheeks.

I wiped them away with my fingers.

The adults prayed that night, and no one slept well. Only the baby, who had no idea of what lay ahead.

Chapter Twelve

In the dense green forest, my family and the families of my relatives, Wa Chong Vang and Shoua Neng Vang, met with Vue Vang. Vue was Nhia Neng's cousin and leader of a group of resistance fighters. He was a muscular man with a broad face and a big nose. He stood a few fingers shorter than Father.

Vue led us to his camp area where makeshift shelters circled an inactive bonfire in the middle. The families there greeted the new ones. As everyone sat on the rough ground around the bonfire, Vue explained to the new families that he and his fighters were known as Chao Fa, a resistance movement against the Communists. The phrase Chao Fa means "Lord of the Sky" in the Laotian language.

The twenty men in Vue's group were former CIA soldiers of General Vang Pao's irregular forces, so they had been here since the General left the country. They joined the Cha Fa to help fight off the Communists because to surrender to the Pathet Lao meant death or torture.

One young soldier said, "I came here because I would rather die fighting than get arrested by the Pathet Lao. I saw what happened to my relative. The Communists arrested him. They cut his flesh and sprinkled it with salt and let him burn in the sun. He screamed and screamed until he fainted from the pain. They also interrogated the prisoners for information and when they got nothing, they kicked and beat the captives with wooden clubs until they were unconscious."

My stomach churned. The war had created monsters. Would the enemy do that to Father if they arrested him? I hoped they'd never find out about his past.

Seven of Vue's twenty men were married, and their families were present. Altogether, including the new families, there were eleven families with children. Vue cautioned that as the group increased in size, it would be harder to keep the children quiet. For our safety, he decided to take the families to Phou Bia, the highest mountain in Xieng Khouang Province in Laos. Phou Bia, a remote area with jungles, would be safe from the Communists. Some former Hmong guerilla soldiers and other Chao Fa groups lived there, and they would protect the families.

Shortly after the meeting, Vue, who had obtained the rifles from the other Chao Fa leaders, provided each new man a rusted carbine rifle. Only four men, including himself, had M-16s. Toua looked braver with a gun in his hands. As a hunter, he knew how to use the weapon.

OVER THE NEXT FIVE DAYS, OUR GROUP PASSED MANY MOUNTAINS and valleys. Climbing densely forested hills with elderly and young children was like digging a tunnel. Their short steps slowed us, and the children cried each time a tree branch whipped them, or they stepped on a sharp object.

We reached the Phou Bia Mountain range one day around noon. The area was a dense jungle with tall, pale-barked, single-trunked trees as top canopy. Teak, Asian rosewood, and mahogany made up the middle canopy. Underneath, the canopies were smaller trees and shrubs.

This place would hide us from the enemy, but we couldn't clear land to grow food. We had to eat what we could find in the wild. We couldn't survive in this remote area for long.

As we rested on the slopes of a mountain range, Vue informed us that a Chao Fa group resided nearby on the slopes of Phou Bia Mountain. Many former Hmong guerilla soldiers and their families were spread throughout the area. The people preferred to stay spread out, so they wouldn't be an easy target for the enemy, who could drop bombs on them at any time.

Each family claimed an area on the hill and cleared it. Weak and exhausted, Grandmother lay on the rough, uneven ground almost lifeless. There was nothing to eat. Father went to hunt, and Mother foraged for edible plants.

I trudged down the hill to the valley for water. At the creek, I gulped mouthfuls, then filled three large bamboo tubes and set them in my basket.

Going up the steep hill with so much weight was difficult. Halfway up, I was out of breath. I heaved a groan each time I took a step. I was exhausted when I reached the camp area. I couldn't imagine hauling water up that hill every day.

In the evening, Father brought a small bird and some ferns. Mother came back with a few wild palm shoots. Grandmother ate the bird, and the family ate the other food.

As darkness closed in, I cuddled beside my grandmother on the hard, uneven ground atop some banana leaves. As usual, I had difficulty falling asleep. My back hurt, and I tossed and turned.

Suddenly, streaks of white lightning broke the blackness. Thunder roared, and gusts of winds whipped the trees. As heavy rain poured down on us, children's cries echoed everywhere. The trees offered little protection. We shivered in our wet clothes and tried to protect seven-month-old Nhia from the noise, wind, and rain. The night seemed to go on forever.

Finally, the rain stopped, and dawn broke, bringing rays of hope. Nhia stopped crying. Father and Toua tried to start a fire, but the wet twigs refused to cooperate. Frustrated, Father split them into small pieces and finally got a fire to start. We huddled around the meager warmth.

When sunlight filtered through the canopy of leaves above, we hung our clothes to dry. People started cutting woods to make shelters. Nobody wanted another night like last night. My family built a lean-to shelter. Ten days later, we finished a small wooden thatch hut with a wild palm leaf roof, close to Shoua Neng and Wa Chong.

Once we were settled, Vue and the other Chao Fa leaders started training every able-bodied man and boy to fight. They trained mornings and hunted and searched for food later in the day.

Every morning when daylight broke, Father and Toua grabbed their rifles and walked out the door. They journeyed to the mountainside for rifle drilling while I stayed behind, my teeth clenched in frustration. I wanted to join them. I was capable, and I needed to learn to fight to protect my family.

My vow to Mother, Der, and Nhia made me want to live up to my name, the sun, the source of all energy that was powerful. I had given up a life in America and education to keep that vow.

One morning, I started the fire early.

"Mother," I said. "I'm going to join the soldiers in their training."

Her mouth twisted, and she shook her head. "No. Girls shouldn't fight. I need you to cook breakfast, get water, and take care of Grandmother and Nhia."

"I'll do the work when I return."

"We're trying to survive." Mother's voice was firm. "We have two men in training. You have things to do."

She took her basket and left to search for food before I could argue. I gulped down my anger. I reminded myself that I was bound to my responsibilities and completing them well would make me a worthy daughter. If doing chores and helping the family made Mother proud, I wouldn't argue and shouldn't be mad.

After Der breastfed Nhia, she gave him to me because as a teenage girl, I had to babysit. When my twin brothers were babies, Der babysat them. Now I babysat Nhia. Der went after Mother. The adults looked for food in the wild.

When the sun climbed high and the shadows grew short, I knew it was noon. I had been studying shadows to pass the time. Mother and Der returned, and I went on my daily trip to the creek for water.

Aside from the rustling of leaves, the day was quiet. A few children sat outside their huts, but they ran inside when they saw me. The children mostly stayed inside when the adults were gone, and though they lived near each other, they were too scared to play together. For now, Phou Bia was a safe haven. But like the children, I couldn't shake the feeling that something ominous approached.

Chapter Thirteen

DECEMBER BROUGHT FREEZING COLD WEATHER. THE temperature in the mountains varied from day and night. The days weren't bad, but the nights were bitter cold. At night, the chill air crawled into my bones and my insides, making me shake. When we breathed or talked, steam came out of our mouths and noses. It was the craziest weather I had ever seen. During the night, Grandmother groaned and Nhia cried. Father put up a fire each night, but nobody slept well.

One evening, Grandmother and Nhia both had a fever. Mother gave them her herbal medicines, but the herbs didn't help. One-year-old Nhia screamed as if he were being pinched and refused to breastfeed. He twisted away from Der and extended his arms to Father. When Father took him, he twisted again and extended his arms to me. I held him tight, rocked and crooned to him, but then he wanted Mother.

My parents prayed and did a *hlawv dab pog,* chanting and chasing the evil spirits away with a burning rag. They did everything they could, but Nhia continued to cry. His face was as red as the cloth that Mother had tied on his neck to keep evil spirits away. Der trembled as tears streamed down her cheeks. My parents and Toua watched with fearful eyes.

We had barely gotten over the twins' death, and now we feared for Nhia's life. This place was safe from the Pathet Lao, but not from Mother Nature and illness. Nhia would not survive long this way.

I couldn't bear another death. I prayed quietly, "Lord of Heaven, Grandfather and ancestors, please take away Nhia and Grandmother's illness, protect them from the cold and save them. Please, please save them."

Father sent Toua to the neighbors. Wa Chong and Shoua Neng came running.

Shoua Neng felt Nhia's forehead and said, "High fever." He started a *khawv koob* and chanted.

Nhia's fever finally broke at midnight, and he grew quiet. Once they confirmed Grandmother's fever was also down, Shoua Neng and Wa Chong left. The adults were exhausted, but they relaxed a little.

Famine had made us all weak. We had been eating two scanty meals a day, and we lacked protein. The edible plants nearby were completely gone. People traveled a long way in search of food.

When the sun rose, Father left, his expression grave. I went out to collect twigs for firewood and stopped near Vue's hut and listened as Father and Vue talked about our problems.

I joined Father on his walk home.

"Father, what are we going to do?" I asked.

"Leave this place."

"Other than this mountain, where is it safe?"

"Nowhere."

We had no more places to run. When the war ended, Chao Fa had been our last hope and Phou Bia Mountain was our only safe place.

At home, Father sat us all down, and said, "The weather

here is not in our favor, and starvation and illness make me worry every day. I shared with Vue that I'd like to gather news about the villages. If it's safe for us to return, I'd like to take the family back to a village. Fong Vang and I will be traveling to the villages tomorrow."

Fong Vang was a young soldier of Vue's. He shared the same clan, so Father treated him as a son.

"Please don't go, son." Grandmother's voice wobbled. "It's dangerous. Your family needs you."

Father's expression hardened. "I'll be quick."

A shadow fell across Mother's face. "Do you really have to go?"

"I must do something. Don't worry." Father turned to Toua. "You take care of the family while I'm gone."

Toua nodded.

My throat thickened as my head generated scenarios of what would happen to Father if he were caught. Why did everything carry such high risks? If Father was caught, what would become of us? Could we survive without him?

Father untied the rope with the machete attached to his waist. To my surprise, he handed it to me. "Keep this knife safe. You understand its importance."

"I'll keep it," Toua said.

"No. I'm worried you might misplace it when you're training," Father said. "Der and your mother will be busy searching for food. Nou only cooks and cares for Nhia and your grandmother. It's better for her to keep it."

The next day after breakfast, Father chanted prayers, then slung his gun over his shoulder. Fong arrived, and they left.

Each day they were gone, I marked the day by chopping a bit of wood off the huge tree in front of our hut. Each time I held the machete, I was curious about the paper hidden inside the handle.

One day, curiosity urged me to take out the paper, and I did.

As I unrolled the paper, words filled both sides. I felt the words with my fingers. Father said he wrote about his involvement in the war, but what else was written here? I longed to read it. Dreams were impossible in the jungle, but the paper reminded me to keep hope alive. I carefully re-rolled the paper and replaced it in the handle.

I marked the tree five times, then ten. Each mark deepened my fear. If something happened to Father, Grandmother would die. She had asked for Father each day and refused to eat. She became so fragile she was unable to turn herself on the cot. Her eyes were sunken. She barely opened them, and her facial bones protruded like a skeleton.

I had never lied to my grandmother before, but I felt I had no choice. I wouldn't allow her to die from starvation.

I cleared my throat. "Grandmother, I heard my father will be here soon. You must eat, so you have energy to talk to him."

"He's almost here?" she said quietly.

"Yes. Now eat."

Grandmother slowly opened her mouth. I fed her mashed wild root, *qos sabyaj thawj*, and gave her water. She finished half the food.

On the evening of the fourteenth mark, Father and Fong finally returned safely. The men crowded our hut, anxious to hear the news. Father's bright eyes showed he had good news.

"The Pathet Lao are asking families in hiding to return. They promise not to harm us. Some families have returned." Father made eye contact with the men around him. "I don't know what you all think, but I'm taking my family back to the village. This is the only way to save my grandson and my mother."

"As your leader, I am advising you that if you think you can live under the Pathet Lao's rules, you are free to leave," Vue said. "I don't want you and your family to suffer more illness and hunger. Our future here is uncertain. I can't say you'd be better off hiding here than surrendering."

Others said they wouldn't turn themselves in.

"Remember the cease-fire agreement. After signing the contract to stop firing, the Communists ignored the agreement and sent troops to wipe out Hmong soldiers," Shoua Neng said. "I don't trust them."

"I'm worried that once people return, they'll arrest former soldiers and resistance fighters," Wa Chong said in his deep voice. "What will you do when you're in their hands? It's easy for them to catch you."

My breath caught in my throat. He had a good point. Maybe it would be best to stay.

After everyone left, Father turned to the family. "This is a tough decision. I'm going to follow my gut. I want to take the risk and go to the village. The Pathet Lao scared me, but I figure it's the best way for the family."

"Thank you, Father," Der said. "This will save my child."

"Your grandmother, too," he replied. "She told me before the war that when she dies, she wants a good funeral with a lot of people, with music of drum and *qeej* to guide her to the ancestral world. She wants a cow killed so she will have an animal to raise in her afterlife. If we stay here, there will be no formal funeral for her."

We all agreed.

"I thought about you," Father said to Toua. "While in the village, I saw a couple of men your age, and I talked to two Hmong leaders who believed you'd be all right there."

"Father, I," Toua hesitated. "I would like to get married before we leave."

I wasn't surprised. He had been talking to a girl who lived on the other side of the mountain.

Father nodded. "You are twenty now. I won't stop you. Bring her tonight. I want to leave soon."

That evening as darkness approached, Toua returned with a beautiful, long-faced woman. Her small nose and thick pink lips made her very attractive. It was no wonder Toua wanted to bring her with him. He introduced the woman as Pa. She was eighteen, the same age as Der.

Father and Vue left to notify Pa's parents of her marriage to Toua. They soon returned. Father told us that Pa's parents were considerate and agreed to postpone the young couple's formal wedding until it was safer, and there was food. Father traded opium with Vue for two silver bars and gave them to Pa's parents as a token of raising Pa. There were no chickens to do a soul-calling for Pa and Toua, so the couple would wait until we reached the village.

Two days later, the people gathered near our hut to say goodbye. Pa's parents came to see her off. Wa Chong and Shoua Neng decided to stay with Vue. They asked Father to send them news of how things were with the Communists.

That morning Father prayed to his father, "Father, today your family is going back to the village to live with the Communist Pathet Lao. If bad things will happen to us on our way or in the village, please make us see a snake blocking our way. I'll take this as a warning not to go on."

Curious, I whispered, "Grandmother, why a snake?"

"In a time of war like this, seeing a snake blocking the path symbolizes danger ahead. Snakes are dangerous."

Father shook hands with Vue and the other men in farewell. The women said goodbye to Mother and wished her well. My father led the way bravely with his machete dangling on his waist tied with a rope. The Communists would kill my father if they discovered he was a former CIA soldier. We could all be killed. No matter the outcome, my father was my hero. He found the courage and took the risks for what he believed was right for his family.

Chapter Fourteen

After six days of traveling, we came upon a hill overlooking a valley with a village. Father pointed to the village and said, "That's Nao Long. We're going there."

We sat underneath a tree. The short tree shadows told me the time was about noon.

"If we come across any soldiers, we put both hands high up in the air." Father demonstrated to everyone and lifted his hands over his head. "This tells the soldiers we're surrendering, so they won't shoot at us."

Too exhausted to speak, we nodded. I hoped we wouldn't meet any soldiers. Who knew what they would do?

Nhia fussed, so Der nursed him. As soon as he finished, Father took Grandmother on his back, and we trudged toward Nao Long. Father led us to the newer of the two subdivisions in Nao Long with new thatch huts.

"All the huts in this section belong to the people who turned themselves in recently. People like us," Father said. "Some are widows whose husbands died in combat. Do you remember Uncle Nao Pao?"

Everyone but Pa nodded. Nao Pao was a neighbor and relative in Thao village who was captured during the attack. He shared the same clan and was in Father's generation, so I called him uncle.

"He lives here," Father said. "The Pathet Lao released him and his family from prison recently. We are going to his hut."

The fatigue in my legs vanished. I couldn't wait to meet him. Maybe Aunty Shoua and my friend Maineng's families lived here, too. I'd find out.

I edged closer to Father. "Father, who lives on the other side of the valley?"

"Hmong Communists. They've lived there for many years."

My heart sped up. "They are our enemy."

"Not anymore," he said. "Now that we surrendered, we'll be safe."

I hoped he was right.

A small river separated the Hmong Communists from the non-Communists. About one hundred huts spread across the non-Communist area. There were fewer huts on the Hmong Communist side. At last, we stopped at one of the thatch huts on the non-Communist side, and Father knocked on the door.

Uncle Nao Pao opened the door. "You all made it here safely!" he shouted. "Come in."

In his late sixties, Nao Pao had grown older. Wrinkles creased his forehead and gray sprinkled his hair. Aunt Nao Pao and Hue, the youngest son, greeted us. The reunion brought hope, and we shed tears of joy.

Uncle told us that during the attack in Thao village, the Communists took them to the border between Laos and Vietnam. The Communists enslaved them for over a year and forced them to work in rice fields from dawn to dusk. They had two scanty meals a day, and they survived only because they had been farmers their whole life.

"The CIA soldiers were killed," Uncle said.

My breath hitched, and I snapped my gaze onto my father. His expression remained calm. I, however, wanted to cry.

We shared Uncle's hut. His nearby neighbor was Aunt Chia Koua, a slender, average-height woman in her fifties, who came to visit. She gave Nhia a round thing that looked like a button.

"It's candy," said Aunt Chia Koua to Der. "It'll melt in his mouth. No worries about him choking."

"Thank you." Der smiled.

Nhia put it in his mouth, chewed, and grinned. We all smiled with him. He wanted another, and Aunt Chia Koua gave him the last one. He clapped his hands, and we all clapped together. In that moment, we felt alive again.

Aunt Chia Koua told us that her husband, Chia Koua, was a former soldier just like Father. He had escaped to Thailand. He left his family behind because he believed peace was coming soon. Once in a while, he came back to visit and brought candies to the children. She had saved a few candies from his last visit.

"Do you know the families on this side of the village?" I asked.

"I know all of them," said Aunt Chia Koua. "I'm searching for my siblings, so I check out every family who comes here."

"Is there a family by the name of Chong Tou Yang?" Der asked.

That was Pheng's father.

Aunt Chia Koua shook her head.

I asked about Maineng's father and Aunty Shoua's husband.

"I don't know them. I don't think they are here," Aunt Chia Koua said.

Disappointment flooded me and I hoped they were safe. Der would never give up hope of finding Pheng. Every night, she wore his ring to sleep, then removed it off in the morning for chores and work.

The following day, we built a hut with the help of our new neighbors. The days stretched out and our fields offered work that kept everyone's mind off the turmoil.

Chapter Fifteen

May 1977

The Communists' ongoing arrests forced us to hide in our fields sometimes for months. For a year, our life on the farms was challenging due to Grandmother's illness, but staying in the fields kept Father safe. Recently, Grandmother became very ill, and we brought her to the village for ritual healings. Shamans and herbalists visited Grandmother in our hut. The emotional support from the community boosted Grandmother's spirit, and her health improved a bit. Nothing was better than being in the village surrounded by friends and relatives. Father said no place was safe anymore, so it didn't matter where we lived. He decided to stay in the village, hoping Grandmother would recover.

I visited Uncle and Aunt Nao Pao and Aunt Chia Koua every day. Being around them made me less anxious and my day shorter. My parents also visited them often. One afternoon as the sun painted the western horizon red and orange, I started preparations for dinner while Der sat with her sleeping child on the bamboo cot. My parents hadn't returned from visiting Uncle. I cleaned the ashes from the mud stove. I started at a knock at the door. I opened the door to find two Communist soldiers, rifles strapped on their backs. My heart sputtered in my chest. What were they doing here? They stared at me and said something, then giggled. What were they saying? I was sure it was about me. Fear tightened my stomach. I wished for magic power to send them away.

As I rubbed my dirty hands nervously, I knew they wouldn't like an unclean girl. I faked a sneeze, "Achoo!" I quickly rubbed my dirty hand across my face, leaving a streak of ashes.

The men chuckled and pushed me aside as they forced their way inside. One man pointed at Der, who stared with wide eyes. The men smiled at her. As they conversed with Der, she shook her head, indicating her language barrier. They seemed to understand and paced around the home.

Then my parents arrived. The men talked in Lao to Father. He translated for Mother that they wanted to take Der to a party they were having in their military camp nearby.

Mother's face twisted in worry. "Tell them that Der is married and has her child to care for."

"They learned from the villagers that Der doesn't have a husband," said Father.

"No one can be trusted here," Mother snarled.

"Father, I don't want to go," Der cried.

Father exchanged dialogue with the soldiers.

"I'm sorry. I can't refuse their authority," said Father quietly. "You must go with

them."

My heart thundered. I did not want to go, but I had promised to protect my sister.

I had to save her. I expelled a big breath. "I'll go," I said.

"No." Der shook her head. "I'll go. I'm older."

"You're only three years older. I'm sixteen now. I can handle this." I tried to sound confident. "Besides, I want to learn the language. Father, tell them that Der's child is not well, and I'll go after I clean myself."

As Father talked to them, I listened carefully to the spoken words to learn them. They seemed to agree. One of them left while the other waited for me.

I cleaned the ashes off my face but purposely didn't comb my hair. The soldier watched me and smiled, showing crooked, yellow teeth. He was short and tan with a flat nose. He was not attractive at all, and his rifle made me nervous. I hated to show my fear, but how could I act normally?

Lately, the Pathet Lao tried to be the villagers' friends just to investigate the people's involvement in the war. The soldiers talked to the men and questioned the whereabouts of the Chao Fa. Every man denied participation in the war and kept quiet about the resistance fighters. Father had made no contact with Vue, Wa Chong, or Shoua Neng since the family left Phou Bia. The Communists wanted to wipe out the Chao Fa.

The soldier walked toward me and spoke a word I took to mean 'go.'

"I'll come to get you later," said Father. "You'll be all right."

I nodded and took a deep breath. I straightened my shoulders. Learning the language was my goal, so I put aside my fear. If I could speak Lao, it would be easier for me to learn to read Lao. It might not be so bad, after all.

As we walked, I cleared my throat loudly on purpose. The soldier looked at me. I pointed my finger at myself and said, "Nou." Then I pointed at him.

"Bane," he said.

I murmured the name. He smiled. I pointed to his shirt, pants, gun, face, nose, eyes, ears, and hair. He told me the words, and I repeated after him.

The party was not too far from the village and not quite near the military camp. The aroma of burnt meat and spices filled the air. My stomach rumbled with hunger. I hadn't eaten anything since lunch. A big bonfire burned in the middle of a large open space. The soldiers who sat around the fire clapped and sang. Two small pigs hung on the poles roasting beside the bonfire. Some soldiers socialized with the girls. I pointed my finger at the pigs, man, woman, firewood, and many other objects. Soon, Bane grew tired of me and left to join the others.

Three Hmong girls mingled with three soldiers. From their laughter, it seemed they were enjoying themselves. I wanted to know their names but kept my distance because I felt safer alone. I moved slowly around, listening to conversations and trying to learn some words.

Two Laotian girls seemed nice and friendly. I joined them. They taught me how to say my name and how to ask for someone else's name. I repeated the words until I could say them correctly and moved on so I wouldn't bore the girls.

When the pigs were cooked, each man sliced a piece of meat with a knife for himself and dug a handful of sticky rice from the bamboo containers. The women ate the leftover ham. I had one small piece and some rice.

The dancing, singing, and drinking started shortly after the meal. Alcohol made many soldiers dance wildly around the bonfire. Some Laotian women danced and sang with them. Like me, the other Hmong girls stood watching. The singers had beautiful voices, but the voices didn't comfort me because anxiety fluttered in my belly.

Later, Bane asked me to dance, and I shook my head. He offered me alcohol, and I refused. He kicked the dirt in frustration. My pulse spiked, sending chills all over my body. I stumbled as I hurried to the path to wait for Father. I wanted to run home, but it wouldn't be safe for a girl to walk in the dark alone. I waited for a long time. Finally, Father came. We left quickly. On the way home, he taught me more Laotian words. He knew the basic language and could write a few words.

The next evening, Bane came again. He chatted with Father by the fire pit but stared at Der, who was cooking rice on the mud stove. Father told him Der's name.

"Der," Father said. "Bane wants you to give him a Hmong name."

"Why can't you give it to him?" Der asked, annoyed.

"He wants you, but I guess I can give him one," said Father.

Father named the soldier Keng, meaning clever. Bane smiled and repeated his Hmong name. I'd call him Lia because he was ugly like a monkey. Good thing he didn't ask me. Soldier Keng's eyes followed Der everywhere. Der avoided looking in his direction. Her hair was as messy as mine, but her beauty still attracted him.

Keng loitered around after dinner and demanded a chat with Der outside. Father told Der to obey, and she went along.

After that, Keng started visiting Der regularly. Father was concerned, but he couldn't stop the soldier because angering him would bring trouble. For Der's safety, the family went back to live on the rice farm, leaving Mother and me home to care for Grandmother. Without Der and Nhia, loneliness filled my heart, but I was happy that Soldier Keng couldn't bother my sister. Hopefully, he would forget about her.

One night as Mother was putting out the fire, a loud knock sounded on the door. Mother motioned me to go to bed. I did and covered myself with my blanket. The door opened.

A man spoke Hmong in a heavy accent, "Hello, Mother. Where's everybody?"

"Well, um...our cousin who lives two huts down the road was sick, and my family has gone to visit him. They'll be back soon. Why are you alone this evening, sir?"

Heavy footsteps walked around the home, and I wondered if he was searching for something.

"Mother, I'm hungry," he said.

"There is rice in the pot. I can give you some."

Silence.

"No," he said. "I want to go to bed with you."

My heart hammered wildly, and my flesh crawled. What could I do if he raped Mother? *Heaven, please send him away!*

"No, you don't want to sleep with me." Mother's voice was firm and loud. "Lord of Heaven sees bad people. He will punish them. You don't want to get punished. And my husband will be home any minute."

The man left. I breathed a sigh of relief. Mother shut the door immediately and came to me. "I'm afraid the soldier might come back. We have to get your grandmother and go to Uncle Nao Pao."

"I hate these Communists," I snapped. "They take our food every month and now they want our women." Anger surged through me. We were so vulnerable. A future seemed impossible with the Communists around. I had a feeling something bad would happen.

In the dark, I carried my grandmother on my back to Uncle's home. She was as light as a load in my basket. My physical strength had grown.

At the rice field the next day, Mother told the family about the soldier. Father's face reddened, and he said, "From now on, we travel and do things together as a family. This is the only way we will be safe. We need to stay away from them as much as possible."

GRANDMOTHER'S ILLNESS GREW WORSE AT THE FIELD. AGAIN, MY parents brought her home for shaman rituals. Mother gathered herbal medicines for her, too, but she didn't improve. After the illness and starvation at Phou Bia, Grandmother was too weak to recover.

Everyday Mother and I took turns cleaning Grandmother in bed, changing her clothes and washing them. I mostly tended to her, and she called for me often until she became mute. For two days she didn't speak. She rarely opened her eyes and couldn't eat or drink.

I washed her face with a cloth and shook her gently. "Grandmother, I want you to eat and drink."

No response. I called again, and her tired eyes opened slightly. She mumbled something. She heard me! I gaped at her in excitement. I'd been afraid she would never speak again.

"Speak louder so I can understand you," I said loudly.

With all her breath, she managed to say, "Thank you…for your…care." She paused. "I bless…you…long...happy life…in good health and prosperity."

"Thank you for your blessing, Grandmother. You can talk now. You'll get better."

"Your…father?"

I hurried outside. My father was splitting firewood down by the chicken coop.

"Father!" I shouted. "Grandmother needs you!"

We rushed inside. Grandmother was lifeless. Father cried bitterly, holding his mother tight against his chest. I stood beside Father in shock and bewilderment. She was just talking. I thought she was getting better.

"Father," I cried, "Grandmother talked to me before I came to get you. Why did she die suddenly?"

He turned to me. Surprise flitted across his features. "She talked to you? What did she say?"

"She gave me a blessing."

He wiped his eyes with his hand. He stroked my hair. "You are the chosen one. It's an honor to receive a blessing from your grandmother or any elderly person who lives as long as she. Keep up your good work. You'll do great in life now that you received her blessing."

A new energy filled me, and I believed him. I just hoped the civil war would stop so I had a chance to shine, to be the daughter I wanted to be, to do the things I loved to do, and to prosper as my grandmother wanted.

We all felt Grandmother's death deeply. I hated that she hadn't seen peace before her last breath. I doubted there would ever be peace. To ease my grief, I reminded myself that she was free at last from suffering. She had lived such a hard life of fleeing war, starvation, and sickness.

Everyone came for Grandmother's funeral. The funeral lasted four days with village people crowding our hut to pay their respects. The men played a drum and *qeej*, a musical instrument, to lead Grandmother on her journey to her ancestor's spiritual world. Father killed a cow for her, so she'd have livestock to raise in the afterlife. Grandmother's wish to die in a village with a decent funeral came true. It was an honor our family had given her. If we had been in the jungle, there would have been no funeral.

Chapter Sixteen

THE WIND WHISPERED IN THE QUIET, DARK NIGHT. EVERYONE WAS asleep, except my parents and me. As always, I was curious about everything and sat with them by the fire pit, listening to their conversations about news in the village. A soft knock sounded at the door. I flinched at the sound. Who would visit this late? I feared opening the door.

A woman said, "Are you still up?"

Father said softly, "Sounds like Chia Koua's wife."

Mother nudged my arm. I jumped up to open the door. Aunt Chia Koua introduced the man with her as Chia Koua, her husband.

"Hello, Chia Koua." Father shook hands with the man. "When did you get back from Thailand?"

"Two days ago." Chia Koua glanced at me. "Are you Der?"

"I'm Nou. My sister is in bed."

"Can you wake her?"

Chia Koua and his wife sat on the stools next to my parents. I woke Der, and she greeted our guests.

"Do you know a man by the name of Pheng Yang?" asked Chia Koua.

Der's eyes widened. "Yes. You know him?"

"He's my nephew, my sister's son."

Der and I gaped at him.

"Pheng is in Thailand," Chia Koua said.

For the first time, I felt as light as air. Thank Heaven and my ancestors he was alive. Der's prayer had been answered. I held Der's hand, and she squeezed mine hard.

"He's been searching all over for you and his child," said Chia Koua. "The last time I came here, my wife told me about you and your son. I told Pheng about your family. He was thrilled to know that you and your son are doing fine."

Tears streamed down Der's cheeks. Chia Koua extended a large, white envelope toward her. "It's from Pheng."

Der wiped her tears with the back of her hands and took the envelope. "Thank you." She smiled.

I hadn't seen that smile for a long time. There was hope for Der and Pheng after all. I couldn't wait to see what was inside the envelope.

"Uncle Chia Koua, when are you going back?" Der asked shyly.

"In two weeks, but I have to go to the woods before dawn tomorrow. I'm a resistance fighter, and I came here secretly."

"Now that you know him, you have to keep your mouth shut." Father's voice was soft but clear.

We all nodded.

"Pheng wants me to take you and your son to Thailand. I'll take the whole family if your father is ready to leave the country."

Der looked to Father. "We must go to Thailand. That Keng soldier scares me. We have to go away from here."

"We will go with you." Father shifted his gaze to Chia Koua. "We'd thought about leaving but hadn't found anyone to lead us. Now we've found you."

"Great," Chia Koua smiled. "Tell no one we are leaving."

For the first time in forever, hope filled me. A future was possible. I laughed softly, light-hearted. Here was my chance to flee the Communists to the country of my dreams.

"Uncle, is it true that refugees in Thailand can go to America?" I asked.

"Yes, if they choose to."

Who wouldn't want to go to America?

Der and I went to bed with smiles on our faces. She opened the huge envelope and took out a letter and the lightweight clothes. The dying fire made it difficult for us to see. Der went through the clothes.

"One shirt for me," she said. "A shirt and pants for Nhia."

I touched each one. The big shirt was soft like a baby's skin. "I wonder what kind of fabric your shirt is. Can't wait to see it tomorrow," I whispered.

"I can't wait to try it on. It feels so good to know Pheng's alive. There is hope for us." Der put everything back in the envelope and hugged it to her as she fell asleep.

When daylight crept over the village, Der and I took the envelope to the stream. She pulled out the white blouse. It had a ruffled front and a golden butterfly pin.

I ran my hands over the blouse, marveling in its softness. "What kind of fabric is this?"

"It must be silk, a special fabric." Der put the blouse on. It fit perfectly.

"You look gorgeous." I smiled. "You should feel special wearing this unique blouse."

Der's dimples deepened. "I want Pheng to see me in this."

"Me, too." I touched the pin. "Is it real gold?"

"Probably not."

"Let's see the letter."

Der took out the letter and looked at it. Her face wrinkled like a dried fruit. "I can't read. How do I know what he's saying?"

Who would read it to us? I couldn't think of a single woman who knew how to read.

"Father can read it," I said.

"Father reading my love letter?" She grimaced. "No."

We fell silent.

An idea flashed in my head. "Father can teach you!"

"I can't learn to read in a couple days."

"Don't have Father teach you everything. Maybe copy a couple of the words from the letter and ask what they are each day. After a few days, you'll know all the words in the letter. Then you can read it to us."

Der grinned. "You are so clever."

Father was eager to help. He went to the military camp and came back with a few pages of paper and a blue pen. On our bamboo cot, Der randomly picked out words to copy. Holding a pen for the first time, she printed each letter so slowly that I lost patience. The printed letters were crooked. I tried to write. I could write faster than Der, but my letters weren't any better. After we had twenty words, we presented the list to our father.

He taught us each word, and we repeated after him. Then, we practiced on our own. After four days, we had learned all the words in the letter.

At the creek, Der read the letter aloud.

August 20, 1977

Dear My Love Der,

I hope you and my son have good health. I almost died from depression. My health has improved since I learned of you both. Your living has given me hope. Thank you for taking great care of our son. I'm sorry I am not there to help you.

My family lives in Ban Vinai refugee camp. Tell your father to come to Thailand. It is safer here. Be careful. The road to Thailand is dangerous.

I know you will look beautiful in the white, silk blouse. I chose white because it's the meaning of your name. You're as beautiful and valuable as silk. The butterfly pin represents me, who wants to be with you forever.

Der, I'm praying for us to reunite. Please wait for me. I'll wait for you. I love you and miss you so much. I can't wait to hold you in my arms. Write to me if you can.

Love,

Pheng Yang

Der hugged the paper tight against her chest. "I love you too." She folded the paper.

"Can I look at the letter?" I asked.

She handed it to me. As I read the letter, the words spoke to me, presenting a message. Astonished, I couldn't stop myself from smiling. I found it unbelievable that a piece of paper with words could talk to me. If I could write well, I could talk to a paper any time I wanted. I could put all the stories I knew on paper, creating books like those I had before. It never occurred to me that I could write my stories for others to read. The new dream of being a writer burst open in my heart. I couldn't wait to get to America! With Chia Koua taking us, we'd be on our way soon. Hope coursed through me, giving me warmth and energy.

The next evening, Father came home with red, puffy eyes.

"What happened?" asked Mother with fear in her voice.

He shook his head as he sat down by the fire pit.

"The Pathet Lao killed Chia Koua and arrested his family," Father said, his voice choked with grief and anger.

Der's eyes bulged like an owl's. I froze, watching our dreams shatter in slow motion. My heart ached. How could we go to Thailand? How could we escape Soldier Keng and the Pathet Lao? As the shock dissipated, thick waves of anger and grief swept over me. I cried my heart out. My family's cries shook the thatch hut.

Toua wiped his eyes with the back of his hands. "Father, how did the Pathet Lao know he came back?"

"The Hmong spies."

"What's the reward for getting your own Hmong killed?" I demanded.

"Money." Father softened his voice to a whisper. "I'm sure other people will flee to Thailand. I'll find out." He paused. "The Pathet Lao leaders mandated a meeting with all the household men. I have to attend the meeting and I need Nou to cook for me, but I want the rest of you to head back to the rice field tomorrow. Nou and I will join you after."

The next morning, Toua, Pa, Mother, Der, and Nhia left at dawn. My anxiety grew as Father and I waited for the meeting. To pass the time, I asked him to teach me Lao, and he did. We practiced conservations in Lao.

Pathet Lao troops of about forty soldiers arrived at noon. They each wore a dark green uniform with a rifle strapped to their backs. Men, women, and a few children stood tall in the field between the two subdivisions waiting patiently for the soldiers to present. Five soldiers stood in the middle of the field while the others guarded the people. Intimidated by the troops, the large crowd remained silent.

A fat soldier talked in Lao for a while before a Hmong man translated.

"Thank you, everyone, for attending this meeting. We believe that you will help us get this job done. No vehicle can travel on the rugged path, so your job is to transport ammunition from other camps to this military camp. The weapons are to protect our families in this village from the enemy."

Their enemies, as I suspected, were the Chao Fa and other resistance fighters. The soldier's chubby cheeks and huge belly made me wonder how he got so fat while everyone else was scrawny.

"We want every family to get involved. You will be scheduled every month. We also want you to be aware of this problem. Last week, six families escaped. We caught and shot them. Anyone who turns against us will be killed."

I held my breath. I wasn't aware of the people who escaped. A murmur swept through the crowd.

"Many of us will be here for a while. Don't be afraid" the interpreter continued. "We are here to protect you. If you see any Chao Fa, you need to report to us immediately. This is the right thing to do. If you don't report, you'll be sent to seminar camps. We hope you understand our concern." The man ended his speech abruptly. He didn't mention Chia Koua and his family.

The crowd dispersed to their huts. Some men whispered about what this meant for their future.

When we got home, I asked softly, "Father, do you know those families that were killed?"

"Yes. The Pathet Lao arrested cousin Neng Chue and accused him of feeding the Chao Fa and of being a former CIA soldier. Neng Chue was innocent, but they took him anyway. The families fled because they were unhappy with the Communists."

That night, I tossed and turned, unable to sleep, as thoughts of the people who'd been killed filled my head.

Chapter Seventeen

November 1977

Father went on a mission for four days. Mother's face was haggard as she constantly paced in and out of the hut. Waiting for his safe return made me restless, too.

When Father finally limped into the hut, I cried in relief. Mother's face showed color. He sat by the fire pit, and we gathered around him.

Father said, "After Soldier Keng mentioned to me that his fellow soldiers killed many resistance fighters and their families, I decided to find out." His voice broke. "I learned that the people at Phou Bia were killed, except a few leaders. Vue escaped the massacre."

My breath caught. Toua's wife Pa gasped. Heaven, her family, my relatives, and the people at Phou Bia Mountain were gone. One massacre after another. I stroked Pa's hair and sobbed. What would happen to us?

"We made the right choice to come here," Mother cried "If we hadn't, we'd be dead like the others."

Father nodded. "The resistance fighters reported that many families were sick with disease, and some died from the yellow rain poison that came from the sky. They believed the yellow rain was a chemical dropped by the Communists to kill the families hiding in the jungles."

Toua jumped to his feet. "They are cruel to do such a thing to our people!"

"Let's not talk about the Chao Fa anymore," Father said. "We can't have any connection with them, or the Pathet Lao will kill us. We must act like we don't care what's going on and that we're good citizens. We must do what we normally do."

How could we go about our normal lives after hearing such news?

The sun hung low in the sky. I took two handfuls of firewood from the heap outside. Soldier Keng walked toward our hut. Anytime we returned home, Keng appeared.

I hurried inside. "Father, Keng's back."

Father stopped working on the arrow bows he'd begun to cut out of bamboo. "Don't worry."

Mother bit her lip. Der picked up Nhia, who played in the dirt by the door.

Soldier Keng joined the family by the fire pit. By now Der and I were familiar with the Laotian language and could follow the conversation. Keng asked Father to marry Der. Father said it would have to be after the New Year, because Der wanted to enjoy the celebration before getting married. Keng seemed satisfied with the plan.

As he stood to leave, Keng pinned Der with a hard stared and told her that if she ran away, he would chase her, kill her, and cut her into three pieces. Der's face turned ashen.

Anger flared inside me, and I suppressed a retort only because he had a gun. Why marry her when he knew she didn't like him? He was a cruel person who just wanted to destroy

Der's life. He picked her because she was a nice, gentle woman. Oh, what a devil!

In the next few days, Father was hardly home, meeting with friends and relatives. One night, he whispered to us that a group of people were planning to flee, but too many Communist soldiers hovered around. We had to wait until it felt safer.

Toua's wife, Pa, was seven months pregnant and feared the journey. Walking in rugged terrain and jungles would be difficult, but for our future and the safety of Der and Father, fleeing was our best option.

Every night I prayed, *Lord of Heaven, my honorable grandparents and ancestors, please protect us. Send the soldiers away. Guard us and lead us to a safe place.*

Chapter Eighteen

December 1977

New Year approached. Everyone, except Nhia, was restless and had difficulty focusing on field work. Every evening, we waited anxiously for Father to come home from his long meetings. Each time he came home, his eyes were dull and empty and his shoulders slumped. We had no escort to guide us to Thailand. Time was running out, and Der cried every night. I wished for magic power to stop Soldier Keng from forcing Der to marry him.

One night, Father came home with a new sparkle in his eyes. We gathered around, and he said, "Finally, we heard from the Moua's cousin, Ger. He and his two Laotian friends will escort us. The price is ten silver bars, one bar from each family. We have ten families. Tomorrow, we'll start to prepare for our long journey."

Der beamed. "This is our chance to go to your father," she told Nhia, who was almost three. "You'll finally meet him."

"Father." Nhia pointed at his grandfather who sat opposite him.

We all laughed, a sweet moment of respite from the constant fear. I wanted to keep the laughter forever.

Pa glanced at her belly. "Toua, I can't go. I won't be able to make a long walk. In about one month, we'll have our baby."

"There's no other choice," Toua said. "If you and I stay, the Communists will know our family has left, and they'll chase and kill them. They might kill us, too. Who knows?"

"Nyab," Father addressed Pa as *daughter-in-law,* "we've thought about your situation. It'll take us probably two to three weeks of walking. If everything goes as planned, you'll have your baby in Thailand. It'll be difficult, but we'll help you."

Pa nodded respectfully to Father, but I discerned the fear in her eyes.

The next day, we all got busy. A year ago, Father had traded opium for a cow. Now he sold the cow for two silver bars. Toua butchered the livestock, while I fetched water for him and cared for Nhia. We killed only half of our animals, so the Communist Pathet Lao wouldn't suspect us of leaving. Toua and I dried the lean meat and wrapped it in banana leaves. We stored the fried meat in the bamboo tubes.

Meanwhile, my parents and sister prepared rice in the field and carried the rice to a hiding place about a day's walk away. The woods would be the starting point of our journey, and we'd need rice.

Finally, after three days of preparation, my family was ready to flee with the others. That morning, we each dressed in two sets of clothes. The dirty, ragged clothes covered the clean ones. On top of our baskets lay hoes, shovels, and knives so it looked like we were going to tend the fields as usual. In the bottom of my bamboo basket was a small blanket, a set of clothes, a canteen, a plastic water tube—not inflated—and two cooking pots.

I strapped the basket on my back and stepped out with no idea what to expect in the coming days. The cold December wind chilled me as I walked around the hut for a final look. I already missed its solid four walls that had protected us from wild creatures.

Mother unlocked the coop door and the pigpen gate, so the chickens and pigs could get out to search for food while we were gone. We hurried past several houses and met a couple on their way to the field. Father told the man we were going to the fields. No one could be trusted to share the truth.

As soon as we were out of the village and into the thicket, we turned southwest toward the forests. We reached the rendezvous around noon where seven families waited for us. Father and Toua quickly joined the men, and they discussed the journey.

Soon more families arrived. One was Uncle Nao Pao's family. Together, we had ten families of eighty people with small children and several elders.

The man from Thailand and his two companions in their late thirties gathered us for instructions. "I'm Ger Moua. I have my Laotian friends, Khamkong and Somsack, to help us. Two important things you need to know before we go. First, all children must keep quiet at all times. One cry could risk everyone's lives."

My breath quickened. How could mothers keep their children quiet all the time?

"I asked each household man to tell the mothers who have small children to bring opium. Did all the mothers bring opium?" asked Ger.

The mothers, including Der, nodded. Father must have told her. Opium would quiet the children. The right amount would put a child into deep sleep. Too much would be deadly.

I was assigned to care for Nhia during the day, so Der could carry rice, search for food, and cook for us. I would never give

Nhia the drug. But how would I keep him quiet? I had a tough job ahead, and it frightened me.

"Second, I'd like some men to be with me up front," Ger said in his deep voice. "I'll provide you guns. This is a dangerous journey, and you must help me watch for the enemy."

Father nudged Mother, and whispered, "I'll volunteer to be in the front line with him."

Her brow furrowed in worry. "No. You can't run fast."

"I have a disability, but I have the experience. This is our journey. It's my duty."

The sun hung high overhead as we formed a line to follow Ger. I strapped Nhia on my back and followed Mother and Der. Pa and Toua followed. Cher Pao Xiong's family took up the rear with Nhia Thong Lee's family in front of us. The Xiong's eighty-year-old grandmother, Youa, and Pa walked without complaining. Nhia and the Lee's five-month-old baby girl slept well.

We walked until the sun dropped behind the mountains, then settled in for the night. The men took turns guarding the group. Somsack rested underneath a tree. He seemed like a nice man to practice Lao with.

I approached him. "Hello."

"Hello," said Somsack.

"I speak a little Lao," I said in Lao. "Can you teach me some words?"

Somsack smiled, showing his nice, white teeth. "Yes."

He taught me words for family, food, forest, and water. I practiced having conversations with him. Owls hooted nearby. A few children started to cry.

"Quiet your children," Ger spoke quietly, and hurried toward the crying children.

Der tried to comfort Nhia, but he continued to cry.

I hurried over. "Don't cry," I whispered to Nhia. "An owl is a harmless bird. I'll tell you a story. You must listen."

Nhia quieted as I told him a fairytale about an owl who tricked the other animals. I told the story with expression, enthusiasm, and a unique voice for each animal. Nhia loved it and wanted another one. I continued to tell him folktales until he fell asleep in Der's arms.

"You are a good storyteller," Der said. "This is why Nhia loves you. Are you as good as Aunty Shoua?"

"No, but I'm trying."

In the darkness, the leaves whispered and crackled in the cold breeze. The five-month-old baby, Mee, wailed.

Ger ran over to the family. "Our lives are at risk," he whispered. "You must quiet her. If she doesn't stop, you have to use opium."

"The drug will kill my child." Aunt Nhia Thong's voice shook.

She wrapped her baby with another layer of blankets and cuddled her tightly. The child's loud cries persisted. Aunt Nhia Thong rocked Mee back and forth and hummed. Soon the infant quieted, but I lay awake for a long time before finally falling asleep.

Chapter Nineteen

We marched cautiously and quietly on the steep, craggy mountain path. Birds sang cheerfully from the tree canopy as if no danger existed and helped distract me from my fear. Still, with every rustle of leaves and grunts or shuffling of wild animals, my heart fluttered.

By midday, Pa and Grandmother Youa's steps got shorter, and our two families fell behind. Youa's grandson, about the same age as me, pulled Grandmother Youa's arm to go faster, making her grunt in pain. If my grandmother were alive, I'd have done the same. As much as I missed her, I was thankful she didn't have to suffer this long, hard walk.

A commotion of loud voices broke out ahead.

"Shoot him! Shoot him!" a man shouted.

We started to back up in a sudden panic. My heart raced.

Tong Pao rushed to us. "Stay calm, everyone."

We stopped our retreat.

"What happened?" asked Toua, his voice edged with fear.

"I'll find out." Tong Pao hurried to the front of the line.

Soon the column began to move again. My heartbeat slowed. A message came down to us that Ger met a Hmong

Communist hunter. Some of the men wanted to kill him, but the hunter begged them to spare his life. Ger set him free, believing he wouldn't betray his own people. I clenched my teeth. Why would Ger trust a Hmong Communist? Hmong spies had killed Chia Koua and many others.

By midafternoon, baby Mee's cries started again. Ger halted the group and walked back to Nhia Thong's family.

"What's wrong with her?" Ger asked. "We can't allow her to make any more noises."

"We are trying to quiet her," said Nhia Thong.

Nhia Thong searched in his wife's pouch and put opium in the infant's mouth. Mee swallowed it and wailed a bit longer. Then she fell quiet and slept.

When the sun went down, we rested for the second night. Mee whimpered, and her father gave her more opium. A few other children cried, and their parents gave them the drug, too. I kept Nhia quiet and interested in my stories. Mother used to scold me for wasting time on stories. But now, those same stories were saving my nephew from a poisonous drug.

At dawn, baby Mee didn't wake up. Her mother sobbed, and Mother did her best to comfort her. Father and Nhia Thong buried the child near our camp area. Just two days into the journey, and already a child's life had been taken. I kissed Nhia as he slept on the banana leaf mat. I would protect him.

Ger reminded the group to keep the children quiet at all times, and the men to keep their eyes and ears open for any sign of Communist troops. I tightened Nhia on my back with the baby carrier. We moved on. A few birds sang quietly. The only noise was our light footsteps on the moist ground.

Bang! Bang! Gunshots exploded ahead. I gasped, heart pounding. The children cried in terror and the adults panicked in confusion. My legs trembled as I turned, not knowing which way to go.

"Move back and run!" someone shouted.

Some people in the front line rushed back while others ran off the trail and down a hill into hiding. People crisscrossed and, in the chaos, some children lost sight of their parents. Their cries echoed through the forest.

The old and weak who collapsed on the ground also called for help. Grandmother Youa was one of them. I wanted to help Grandmother Youa, but Nhia was crying on my back and my family shouted for me to run. I froze.

"Nou, hurry!" Toua ordered. "This way!"

Grandmother Youa's grandson returned for her, and I broke from the grip of terror. I ran down the hill at full speed, following Toua. Mother and Der weren't far ahead.

We ran for our lives, spreading out between trees and bushes and stepping on everything in our way. The murderous ground ripped my cheap sandals and bit my bare feet.

"You hurt me," cried Nhia as I jostled him in my race to keep up with Mother and Der.

"I'm sorry." I panted. "Please don't cry. The bad people are after us and Aunty has to run."

Tree branches whipped our faces. Nhia cried out again.

"Stop crying!" My lungs burned in my chest.

When the gunshots finally stopped, I halted and put my hands on my knees to catch my breath. When I looked up, I realized that Mother, Der, and I had lost Toua, Pa, and Father.

"We've lost the others," I gasped. "How can we find them?"

"They can't be far," Mother panted. "They'll find us."

Der took Nhia off my back, and we collapsed beneath a tree exhausted. She checked Nhia's body for any wounds. Like everyone else, he had scratches on his arms and legs. Our feet bled from stepping on rocks, twigs, and thorns. The baby carrier had left red, painful marks on my shoulders.

"I'm sorry you are hurt, Nhia." I smoothed his hair. "I love you and didn't mean to hurt you."

"It's all right," Der said.

Deathly quiet settled around us. It seemed the creatures were as frightened as the hunted people and had gone into hiding. My body ached, but fear kept me from resting.

I stood. "I'm going to find Father, Toua, and *tis nyab*." I called Pa '*tis nyab*', meaning sister-in-law.

"Be careful." Haggard fear shown on Mother's face. "If you don't find them nearby, come back."

I had no knife to mark the trees so, as I ventured up the hill, I collected dried twigs and made crosses on the ground to mark my way. The rustling leaves tightened my nerves and adrenaline pumped through me.

"Be strong," I murmured. "I can do this. I am Mother's son. Be brave like a man."

I paused and took several deep breaths. Where could I find them? Yesterday, Father told us, *"If we're separated, whistle and call the person's name."*

I moved quietly and whistled softly, "Toua? Father? Where are you?" I whistled every so often as I crept through the jungle.

The sun climbed higher.

Finally, I heard a whistle. "Nou?"

"It's me." I whistled back. "Where are you?"

"Over here."

I picked my way cautiously toward the sound and found Toua and Pa underneath the shrubs. Relief flooded me, and I burst into tears.

"Not so loud," Toua said. "Where is the family?"

"They're down there." I pointed. "Have you seen Father?"

Toua shook his head. I led the way while Toua supported Pa as we headed to where Mother, Der, and Nhia waited.

Mother and Der's eyes glistened with tears when we reached them.

"You found them, my brave girl," said Mother. "I'm proud of

you." Tears welled in my eyes. Mother studied Toua and Pa. "Thank our ancestors you are all right."

"I'm worried about Father," Toua said. "I'll go find him."

I scanned the sky. Though the trees blocked the sun from a clear view, the angle of shadow was growing. "I'll go with you," I said. "We should eat first."

Mother had dropped her sack of rice, but Der had hers, along with the food we had packed that morning. We sat beneath the tree together. Mother unfolded the rice and fried chicken from the banana leaves and gave us each a portion.

"Toua, where are Father's bow and arrow he gave you?" I asked.

"I'm sorry, I ran into a tree branch, and they broke. I threw them away."

I stopped chewing my food. That meant no hunting. No meat. Der's sack of rice would last us maybe three more days. Our journey would take two weeks or more.

Toua explained that while running, Pa slipped and fell on her back. Luckily, she didn't fall on her stomach. Toua had kept her hidden in the nearby dense shrubs. The enemy passed them in search of survivors, and they stayed hidden until I found them.

After we ate, Toua and I followed the trail back to the shooting. We hid behind trees as we went, checking our surroundings. When we neared the place where everyone had scattered, we waited behind trees to make sure no soldiers were around. When all remained quiet, we hurried the rest of the way to the site.

I had to force back tears when we found two dead bodies, a woman and a boy. Farther up, we found more bodies. My skin crawled and my heart pounded. We picked our way through the area and found Ger's body. He'd been shot in the head and neck. I trembled. Not too far from Ger, we found another body, and my heart stopped.

Father.

Heaven, why? It was my worst nightmare. Father had been shot in the chest. Blood covered his shirt. I dropped to my knees beside him, vision blurred, grief and anger boiling inside me.

"Father, I'm so sorry you had to die like this," I cried softly.

"No time for crying." Toua's voice was taut. "Take Father's knife."

The barong machete was in its case with the string still tied to Father's waist. I tried to untie the string, but my hands shook too much.

"Take out the knife and cut the string." Toua picked up Father's gun and went to look for Ger's. He came back with two guns and a knife.

I had my father's knife.

"Hurry, we need to dig a hole to bury Father," said Toua.

He used the knife like a shovel and pried up dirt. I used the machete. My hands and arms ached with each puncture into the ground. I scooped the clay dirt out with my hands.

We dug a shallow hole and buried Father. I put the machete in its case and tied the string around my waist. This was my treasure, the only memory of my father. I sat on the ground and rested my head on the dirt pile, my father's grave, and sobbed. Toua gently pulled my right arm and coaxed me to stand.

His eyes shimmered with tears. "We must find our way back before it's dark," he whispered.

I didn't want to go. Leaving my father alone in the dirt felt like a dagger stabbing my heart. "Goodbye, Father," I managed. "Rest in peace. I love you."

Grief and fear drained my strength. I wasn't sure if I could make it back. "Toua, can you get me a walking stick?"

He found two sticks, one for him and one for me. Toua led

the way bravely. I wanted to be more like my brother, to just move on. It seemed easy for him.

At the hideout, Mother jumped to her feet and greeted us. She took one look at our faces and sank to the ground. Her eyes closed and it seemed as if she had fainted. Der quickly gave Mother her canteen of water. Mother shook her head. Der opened the canteen anyway and poured water into her mouth. After Mother gulped a mouthful of water, she looked up at the sky.

"Wa Shoua, don't leave me," she cried. "I need you. You're my leader, my everything, my life."

She buried her face in her hands. She sobbed so hard, her whole body shook. Der and I wrapped our arms around Mother. Toua and Pa did the same. We all cried as one. Without Father, the leader and protector of the family, the darkness threatened to overtake us.

Night fell. Nhia slept, but we all stared into the shadowy night. Every fallen nut, every moving branch or animal noise startled me. I had been afraid before, but without Father, I was terrified.

I whispered, "Mother, do you have any idea where we'll go from here?"

"I think we should go back to the village."

"We'll try to find the survivors," said Toua. "If we find some of the men, they might know the way to Thailand. I want to search for them first thing tomorrow."

I relaxed a little. Toua had a plan.

Chapter Twenty

Toua led us courageously on the rugged path toward the valley. He planned to look for a stream or creek. If we could find one, there was a possibility we'd find other survivors. I was proud of my brother for taking on my father's role. I wasn't born as tough as him, but I'd watch him and learn. Father always said that learning came from observing and doing. I tried not to think of Father, alone and in the jungle. He would want me to stay strong so I could take care of my family.

In the valley, we found a creek. We rested and cooked rice with the fresh water. After we ate, we traveled along the creek in hopes of finding other scattered families.

As we walked, Toua whistled softly, "Anyone nearby? I'm Toua Vang."

After several attempts, someone whistled in response. We hurried forward and my heart soared when we found Tong Pao and Uncle Nao Pao's families unharmed. We were all relieved to see each other. The men gathered together and talked about what to do. The women listened.

Toua and Tong Pao, a tall, muscular man in his late forties, agreed to go farther down the creek to look for more families.

While they were gone, the rest of us collected firewood and prepared dinner.

That evening, Wa Meng and Youa Cho Moua's families joined our group. Wa Meng and Youa Cho, in their late fifties, were brothers. They told everyone that Ger Moua, their cousin, was the first to die during the shooting. The enemy killed Youa Cho's wife and his youngest son. When the brothers fired their carbines at the enemy, the Communists had backed off quickly.

Wa Meng believed the Laotian men, who had disappeared, ran off to the nearby Communist village for safety. He didn't think they collaborated with the Pathet Lao. Wa Meng suspected it was the Hmong hunter who told the Pathet Lao troop about the group.

"Do you truly believe it was the Hmong hunter?" I asked.

"Yes," said Wa Meng. "Who else would have known? If Ger had killed him in the first place, this wouldn't have happened."

There was no proof, but the hunter was the only one who had seen the group. It could have been him. I wondered about Soldier Keng. Maybe he found our hut empty and chased us. Could it have been him? I wanted someone to blame and hate. I picked up a stick and jammed it hard in the dirt. If I could, I would kill them both.

Half the families were missing. I wanted to ask more questions, but proper women weren't supposed to get involved in men's meetings. I also wondered what happened to the Laotian smugglers. Had they really abandoned the group, or were they wounded?

ON THE THIRD DAY AFTER THE SHOOTING, THE MEN GATHERED TO sketch out the next plan while the women and children listened nervously. I sat behind Toua. Each adult man took a turn to voice his opinion.

"We have two choices." Toua took the lead. "We either return to our village or continue on to Thailand ourselves, although none of us know the way. Both choices have danger."

Lue, Wa Meng's oldest son, said, "We want to get to Thailand, but if no one knows the way, then we must return. If we beg the Pathet Lao and promise to be good citizens, they might spare our lives."

Youa Cho nodded. "The Communists are everywhere, and many villagers are spies. If we don't know a safe route to get to Thailand, we don't stand a chance."

"I understand your reasons," said Uncle Nao Pao. "But I'm a former prisoner. Returning to the Communists will mean severe punishment, if not death. Can you work from dawn until dusk and tolerate being beaten every day?" He shook his head. "Not me. I'd rather die."

"One good reason to go back is that we know the way home," said Wa Meng.

Tong Pao said, "You all have good reasons. Either way is not good."

The men continued debating.

"Can I tell you what I think?" I managed to ask.

"Go ahead," said Tong Pao.

"I think we'd be better off going to Thailand."

Toua agreed. Some men discussed *saib taw qaib*, a ritual where a chicken is killed and boiled whole and the feet and eyes are used to determine fate. But we had no chickens, so the ritual was impossible.

Tong Pao was a revered shaman and had his *kuam*, a divination tool made of a bull horn. The men decided to use that, and this was the first time anyone had used the *kuam* on a situation like this. They hoped the divination tool would help them reach a conclusion and ease their minds. The *kuam* is a spiritual relic used to determine agreements between the shaman and the spirits. It is also used during a soul calling ritual.

Tong Pao took the *kuam* from his black shaman bag. He held the pair of cut-split horns in his hand as he murmured to the spirits of the Earth, his ancestors, and his parents. Tong Pao asked the spirits to make the pair both face up if going to Thailand was safe and a better choice. He tossed the *kuam* on the ground. Everyone watched. Both horns faced down, crossing over one another.

Fear flashed over the adults' faces. Tong Pao shook his head and picked up the *kuam*. He murmured again. This time he asked if going back to the village was safe and a better choice. He tossed the *kuam*. It was the same result. The women's faces turned ashen. A few men shook their heads. The terror in my belly intensified. We were trapped. What would happen to us?

"As you see, neither option is good," Tong Pao said in a tight voice.

The ambiguous reply from the *kuam* left us all uneasy. Some wanted to move on while others felt the group should return.

I turned to Der and whispered, "What do you think?"

"I want to go on." Der's voice was soft and shaky. "I can't return to face Keng. He'll kill me."

"You're right," I said. "I don't know what's ahead, but I don't want to return either."

I leaned on her shoulder as the debate raged.

Finally, the men decided to move on. We'd head west, the direction Ger had been leading us. Der's face brightened. I shared her relief but feared the journey ahead.

The next morning the five families of thirty people started off again. The column was smaller and quieter. Our challenge was finding our way to Thailand.

Two days later, we came upon a village. We skirted around it, hoping to go unnoticed. We stopped at noon to cook the edible plants, ferns, and vines that we had gathered along the way while our men patrolled the area.

Before long, Lue and Toua appeared with their rifles,

escorting two Laotian men. I recognized one of the men. He was Khamkong, Ger's friend. Wa Meng spoke harshly to Khamkong in Lao.

Tong Pao translated for the women. "Khamkong said his partner, Somsack, was injured at the shooting and he took Somsack home. He didn't mean to abandon us. He's here with a new guy to take us to Thailand. It's hard to trust him, but we don't have a choice. I think we are still safer with him leading us."

The women nodded.

"Mother, I need a silver bar," said Toua.

"We already paid them so much money! Why do they want more?" snarled Mother.

"They are demanding more money, and we have to pay the new guy."

"I hope they don't intend to rob us and leave," she muttered.

Toua hesitated. "I think they'll escort us."

Mother frowned as she slowly untied her waist pouch and took out the last silver bar we got from selling the cow.

The group paid the Laotian men four silver bars.

That night, the Laotians guarded us, checking our surroundings for the enemy. Their presence eased everyone's fear that the *kuam* had presented an ambiguous answer. I had faith in the Laotians. I felt our ancestors had sent help, and we would reach Thailand safely. We would continue the journey the next morning.

Chapter Twenty-One

MIDAFTERNOON APPROACHED WHEN WE FINALLY REACHED PHU Hau, a mountain near the Mekong River. At the top of the mountain, we rested. Each household man cleared a spot between the trees for his family for the night. The Laotian men took off to locate a safe route to the river.

Gusty winds whipped at the top of Phu Hau. The treetops thrashed and we feared they would come down on our heads. Little sunlight pushed through the dense canopy. It had been twenty days since we left our village. Along the way, three children had died from starvation and opium poisoning. According to the men, in one more day, we would reach the Mekong River, the longest river in Southeast Asia. It divided Laos and Thailand. On the other side was our country of safe haven. Freedom was within reach. Most adults whispered excitedly to each other. Even the faces of the grieving parents who had lost their children started to show color.

Like everyone, I hadn't eaten since morning. The two scanty meals we ate daily barely gave me the strength I needed. My exhausted body begged me to sleep, but I couldn't. Nhia slept on my lap and arm, and I had to keep an eye on him while Der and Mother searched for food. I ruffled his hair and grinned. He had made it to the Thai and Lao border. He was starving and as light as a stick. Every grain of rice that we saved for him had helped keep him alive. Nhia was handsome like his father. Soon Der and Nhia would meet Pheng, and he'd feed and nurture them. Thinking about their new life gave me energy.

Pa lay on the ground with her belly as round as a melon. Starvation and her swollen, painful legs and feet deteriorated her strength. Still, excitement sparkled in her eyes.

The Laotians returned a short time later. They told us that the village by the river valley was probably occupied by the Communists. Crossing the village and the Mekong River would be dangerous. The Laotians had to find a safe path around the village to the river. The news frightened us, but we had hope in the Laotians to lead us safely to Thailand.

When darkness approached, Der checked Nhia's pulse as she did every night. She wrapped him tighter in the blanket. Everyone lay on the hard, cold ground for the night. The children no longer cried. They were either too weak from starvation or drowsy from the opium.

The wind in the pine trees whistled loudly, keeping me cold and awake. I gazed at the one bright star that showed through the canopy and imagined the star was watching me and saying good night.

I spoke through chattering teeth, "Heavenly star, do you know that we are starving and dying? Please help us get to Thailand safely." I watched the star until my eyes grew heavy, and I fell asleep.

As soon as daylight broke, Toua went to meet with the other men.

When he returned, he said, "The Laotian men left to check

on a safe route for us. They want to make sure the farmers are out of the fields near the river before we cross their farms."

"Good," said Mother. "We paid them so much money. They need to ensure we're safe. Is there a way to go without crossing the fields?"

"They are looking into it."

"When are they coming back?" she asked.

"They'll be back by noon or evening so we can leave during the night."

"Noon or evening," I murmured.

I'd study the tree shadows, and the sunlight that filtered through the canopy to tell time.

For breakfast, Der boiled the wild palm shoots that she and Mother had gathered the night before. Toua set aside a small ration of the food and prayed to our ancestral spirits for their protection. In the wild and in a dangerous situation, it was important to pray to them at every meal. I tasted a bit of the cooked shoots and spat them out. The bitter taste made me grimace. I had eaten bamboo shoots, fern, and tender vines with salt during the trek. The wild palm shoots didn't taste like food. I drank water from my canteen.

"Nou, you must eat," said Mother. "We have to eat anything available to us."

"I'll try later." I wished I could eat anything like my sister.

When the sun sat above the treetops, the people who had gone foraging for food came back, and everyone waited anxiously for the Laotian men. Midafternoon approached, and we waited. The sun disappeared, and still no sign of the Laotians.

Although it wasn't his turn, Toua helped the other men patrol through the quiet night.

At sunrise, the men bustled around the camp looking for signs of the Laotians while the women and children gathered in the middle. We were all scared, imagining the terrible things our guides' absence might mean.

The Laotians still had not returned at sunset. We'd seen no soldiers and heard no gunshots. Where could they be?

At last, Toua joined the family. He wore a cloudy expression. "The men and I think the smugglers abandoned us." His voice was thick with disappointment and anger.

"I never trusted those people," Mother muttered. "I had a feeling they were just after the money."

My stomach clenched. "We've been tricked." I squeezed my eyes shut and tried not to cry. How foolish we were to trust them. Weren't there any good people left in the world?

"What are we going to do?" Der whispered.

"Tong Pao and Youa Cho volunteered to go down to the valley tomorrow to find a safe route," Toua said.

"Brave men," Der murmured. "We are so close."

I put my hand on my sister's shoulder. "Pheng's waiting for you and Nhia."

She nodded.

At dawn, the men met again among the trees. Most of the children were still asleep. Too weak to walk, Tong Pao's five-year-old son Song crawled toward the meeting.

"Father, come back," he said breathlessly.

Tong Pao picked him up. "I'll be back to take you to Thailand."

"I'll rest there." Song pointed to his mother. "Until you come to wake me up."

Tong Pao hugged his son. Tears welled up in my eyes. I hoped for Tong Pao's safe return. Like me, Song couldn't eat wild palm shoots. If I didn't have some vine leaves to eat, I'd be like Song, who barely had enough energy to move. Song was the youngest child in the Lor family, and his father had carried him on his back the entire trek. He fed Song and rubbed his back to get him to sleep. Sometimes he told Song fairy tales, and they laughed together when Tong Pao came to a funny part.

Since Song had grown so weak, Tong Pao had shown great concern. He had searched for food and water for the family and the group, and now he was risking his life to find a safe route for us all.

After the meeting, Tong Pao and Youa Cho left. We all prayed for their safe return. Mother and Der went to scavenge for food with other women. The sun rose above the canopy. Toua and the other men paced. I held Nhia on my lap and hummed softly to him.

Pow! Kapow! Gunshots exploded in the valley. Nhia and I rushed to Pa nearby. Mother, Der, and the others ran back. A few children clung to their mothers and cried. Toua ran around telling the women to quiet their children. Soon we fell silent, still like the trees.

Evening arrived with no sign of Tong Pao and Youa Cho.

Song's cries echoed softly nearby. Toua and I went to check on him. He trembled on his mother's lap.

"Big brother, is my father coming back?" He spoke barely above a whisper.

"I'm not sure." Toua picked up Song. "We'll have to wait until tomorrow and see."

"Don't go anywhere until he comes back," said Song quietly. "I don't want him to miss us."

Toua nodded.

"I'll sleep until my father comes to wake me up." Toua's eyes overflowed with tears. He turned away and quickly wiped his eyes with the back of his hand.

I reached for Song's bony hands. "You must eat so you can go to Thailand."

"I can't eat palm shoots or insects. I'll eat rice when we get to Thailand."

My heart broke for Song, Nhia, and the other fragile children. Song had been an energetic and talkative boy, but now he could barely walk or speak.

Tong Pao and Youa Cho didn't return. Song rested in the area where he had told his father he'd wait. No one could make him eat or drink.

Chapter Twenty-Two

SONG LAY FLAT AND COLD ON THE GROUND WHERE HIS FATHER had left him. His broken-hearted mother sobbed quietly. There was no funeral, no ritual to send him to his ancestor's world. We buried him immediately.

I had witnessed many deaths, and each one had scarred my heart and drained my strength, hope, and dreams of a future. My heart was so wounded that I had no tears for Song's death.

Six days in Phu Hau seemed like an eternity. Nhia had lost interest in stories and slept most of the day. Mother, an herbalist, was well prepared with her medicines, but the children weren't dying of sickness. They were dying of starvation and opium poisoning. Pa had been having difficulty breathing. She whimpered often because she feared losing her unborn child, and she feared for herself, as well.

Wa Meng and Toua had crept down the mountain and climbed treetops to check for any activity going on in the valley. Each day, they reported seeing farmers tending their fields. It wouldn't be safe to cross the valley even under cover of darkness.

Toua stayed up late into the night. He woke up when people

sneezed or coughed. When there were cracking sounds, he'd snatch his rifle, scaring everyone. He became scrawny and his face gaunt.

The tenth day felt like ten years.

It was late afternoon when Toua and Wa Meng returned from scouting a safe route. They gathered us all together.

"We found a rice field that has been completely harvested, and we didn't find anyone there for the two days we watched," said Wa Meng. "There are woods on the other side of the field by the river. Our plan is to move down near the rice field and wait there until dark to cross the field."

"Once we cross to the wooded area, we'll have a good chance," Toua added. "We're planning to leave tonight."

Everyone's eyes lit with hope. It was a risky plan, but it still felt as if we were being released from a dark hole and daylight was our reward.

"Hopefully there will be no moon," said Wa Meng. "The field has no trees to protect us."

"If you have something to cook, make sure to do it early, before we leave," said Toua. "We need all our energy for tonight."

Der cooked the banana shoot that Toua had found while scouting. Unlike the bitter wild shoots, the banana shoot had a sweet taste that I was able to swallow. We had a decent meal that evening. It gave us needed strength.

As the red and orange streaks of evening lay against the sky, Toua chanted to the spirits of Father and our ancestors. He asked for their protection. Mother prayed, too.

Getting ready to leave, I tied my canteen full of water and the machete to my waist and carried the basket that had a blanket, water tube, and a pot. Der carried Nhia with the baby carrier.

Toua and Wa Meng led the group. I walked with Pa to help her while Mother walked with Der and Nhia. The cold air chilled us as we picked our way down the rugged mountain path to the valley.

Nearing the terraced rice fields, dogs started barking nearby. We halted and sat on the ground without making a sound. Thankfully, the children remained silent, some from opium. One cry could mean our deaths.

When the barking finally stopped, my legs were cramped from sitting too long on the rough ground. Toua and Wa Meng circled us, reminding us in whispers to take caution as we crossed the fields.

I felt uneasy stepping down the uneven, terraced rice field. We needed the cover of darkness, but it was difficult to see. Through the quiet night, we crept cautiously among the dried rice stalks.

Chapter Twenty-Three

The field seemed endless. After a while, a message reached me that we were halfway through the field and needed to speed up. I passed the message to Pa and the person behind her. Soon the people behind Pa and me hurried past us.

"Can you walk faster?" I whispered.

Pa grunted in pain, but she quickened her pace only a little. She was doing her best and couldn't go any faster. In the darkness, we fell behind, and I could no longer see the others. My heart pounded.

I whispered, "I have to carry you so we can keep up with the group."

"How?"

"Put your back against mine."

I took off my basket. Our backs touched. We linked our arms. I crouched and dragged Pa, sucking air into my burning lungs. The pain in my back surged with each breath and step. Pa's groans persisted.

At last, we caught up with the rest of our group. Another message came to us that we were near the woods by the river. I could smell freedom. By midnight, we should reach Thailand.

Suddenly, dogs barked, and gunshots flashed. I tripped and fell to the ground with Pa on top of me. I nearly choked and gasped for air. Pa moaned and rolled over to the side. My heart hammered. Cries of terror broke the night. Some people collapsed on the ground while others ran.

"We must run," I said, panting.

"I can't," Pa cried. "You go."

"Father," I prayed, "please protect us and help us get out of here."

Gunfire continued all around us in a deafening roar.

"Pa—Nou, where are you?"

I barely heard Toua call our names.

"Over here," I cried.

Toua stumbled over to us, a dark shadow in the night. Keeping low, he grabbed Pa under her arms and began dragging her. "Follow me!" he ordered.

I pushed to my knees. "Where are Mother and Der?" My voice trembled as badly as my body.

"I don't know. We'll find them later." He spoke fast with fear.

I wouldn't leave until I knew Mother, Der, and Nhia were safe. I watched the direction of bending rice stalks, so I could follow Toua and Pa later. Then, I crawled slowly beneath the gunfire, searching for Der and Mother. I found black figures lying on the ground and touched them. Some were dead, others moaned in pain. Dread and grief wrapped me tight, and I shuddered.

A pained cry drifted my way. Was that Mother? I gasped for air and again prayed, "Father, help me. Give me strength and courage." I took a deep breath and crawled toward the sound.

"Mother?"

"Der was shot," she said on a sob.

My heart stopped.

Chapter Twenty-Four

Der lay on the ground with Mother at her side. Nhia cried weakly in Mother's arms. I knelt and embraced my beloved sister. Our foreheads touched. Der moaned. Sorrow gripped my heart, shaking me and sucking the life out of me.

"You'll be all right," I sobbed, but my eyes had no tears. I smoothed her hair. "I'm taking you to safety. Get on my back."

"Don't," Der managed to say. "Take...my son...to his father. The ring...too."

"You are coming with us." I tried to lift her but couldn't. My hands slid in the warm blood on her side.

"Go... before it's... too late," Der spoke breathlessly. "Go...."

"No! You must come with us. Nhia needs you! Pheng's waiting for you!"

"Please," she begged, "save my...son."

I had to save them both. I wanted to stop time and reverse everything.

A bullet flew past, too close. Panic rose in my chest. Der was right. I had to leave and take Nhia and Mother with me or we would all die.

"Der, I love you. I want to be your sister again in the next life," I sobbed. "I will do everything in my power to bring Nhia to his father."

"Can you help raise…him?" she choked out the words.

"Yes." I nodded. "I will."

Gunfire continued around us, and I hoped she could hear me. I felt for her fingers and slipped the ring off her too-skinny finger. I slid the ring onto the rope holding the machete. Quickly, I fastened the rope on my waist and retied it.

"Goodbye, Der." I squeezed her hand and swallowed hard. I hated life. I hated the world that destroyed my family.

"I love you, Der," Mother wept. "We'll be mother and daughter again."

I fought to keep from lying down beside Der and dying with her. I forced my voice to be strong and said, "Mother, can you walk?".

"Yes."

I carried Nhia on my back and searched for the trail of bending rice stalks to Toua and Pa but darkness made finding the trail impossible, so we were forced to pick our way toward the woods. Leaving Der to die and without a grave ripped my heart into pieces. An ocean of grief sucked all my strength. My mother pulled my arm to go faster, but I couldn't. I wanted so badly to take a bullet and die with Der. Nhia's grunting brought me back to my senses. The child was alive, and I must bring him to his father as I had promised. I quickened my pace. The gunfire continued, but not as close and, by the time we reached the woods, quiet had returned. Mother and I stopped beneath a tree to catch our breaths. Mother groaned softly.

Fear gripped me. "Mother, are you hurt?" I demanded.

"A bullet went through my left arm."

Oh Heaven! My heart leapt into my throat. I reached for her arm. Warm blood had soaked through the long sleeve.

"Nhia was wounded, too," she said. "I don't know where."

It was too much for me to take. How could I save them? A

boulder seemed to press down on my chest. I wanted to scream, to cry, to curse the people who did this. But now wasn't the time. I swallowed my emotions and drew in several deep breaths and told myself that we'd be all right. I could take care of them. I had to.

I felt Nhia's body for his injury. He grunted when I touched his right arm. He was bleeding but not as much as my mother.

"Mother, did you get shot while you were with Der?" I asked.

"Yes." She lifted her good arm. "Tear my sleeve to cover Nhia's wound."

I tore the top of the clean sleeve and wrapped the fabric around the spot on his arm wet with blood. Then, I took off one of my shirts and wrapped it around Mother's wound. Hopefully, the make-shift bandage would stop her bleeding. The December air chilled me, but it wasn't as cold as the time we were at Phou Bia Mountain. Still, Mother shivered.

"Mother, are you cold?"

"Grieving," she replied through chattering teeth.

I stroked her hair and remembered Grandmother's advice. "Take deep breaths," I said. "Don't think about Der right now. You have me and Nhia. We are grateful we still have you. We'll be all right."

The words were easy to say but hard to believe. She took several deep breaths and slowly stopped moaning.

After the short rest, we continued deeper into the woods. A low sound echoed nearby. We paused to listen. The sound was familiar. We moved closer and listened again—it was Pa moaning.

"Toua, is that you?" Mother whispered.

"Yes. We're here."

A heavy weight lifted off my shoulders. My brother! I was no longer in charge. We found our way in the dark to them. As we sat, Pa touched my hand.

"Is everyone all right?" Pa whispered.

"Mother was shot in the arm, and I wrapped the wound with my shirt," I said, as I put Nhia on my lap.

"I'm sorry, Mother," Toua said. "I'll look at it tomorrow. Where's Der?"

"She-she didn't make it," Mother said through sobs.

Pa burst into tears, and Toua hushed her. Mother wheezed and trembled. I smoothed her hair. I wondered if Der was free of pain now or still suffering. A soft cry escaped my mouth, and I tried to choke back my grief.

"It's hard." Toua's voice wavered. "But we must forget the dead and focus on getting to safety. We must be strong if we want to live."

Toua and Father were good at coping. I had to try to be like them. I sucked in a deep breath and kissed Nhia.

We waited impatiently for daylight. Before the attack on our village, I had loved nighttime because I could sleep and was free from labor. Now I hated the night. My exhausted body demanded rest, but my eyes refused to close, my brain replayed terrifying images, and I couldn't stop thinking about Der. Thankfully, Nhia slept.

When the trees at last became visible, Toua looked at Mother's arm. "It looks like the bleeding stopped. You need to see a doctor when we get to Thailand." He stood. "I'm going to check on the river. Wait here."

"Be careful," Pa said.

"Don't wander around," Toua said. "The Communist village is not too far, and we can't have any farmers see us."

"I have to look for herbs for my wound. I won't go far," said Mother.

Toua scratched his head. "Sorry, I don't know what they look like."

"I'll go with you, Mother," I said.

"No. You have Nhia and *nyab* to look after." Mother's voice and face showed pain.

I should be the one searching for herbs to heal her, but like Toua I knew nothing about herbs.

"Drink some water before you go." I pointed to my canteen by the tree.

Mother took it with her good hand, drank a mouthful, then set the canteen back against the tree. She and Toua left.

Pa changed position and groaned. I lay Nhia, who still slept in my arms, beside Pa. I checked Pa's ragged pants. She'd scraped her thighs. Her buttocks were bruised with minor cuts.

"*Tis nyab,* I'm so sorry," I said.

"I'm glad I'm not dead. Toua saved me and our child." Pa released a thick breath. "I'm afraid this child may be coming soon."

Panic blasted through my nerves. I shook my head. "No. Please no. Not in this place."

"Hopefully, we'll cross the river tonight, and I'll have the baby tomorrow in Thailand," Pa said in a strained voice.

"Yes. Tell the baby to wait until we're in a safe place."

I wished we could tell the child to wait. We had to get out of this place soon. I couldn't endure anymore deaths. Too many scars already covered my heart.

Chapter Twenty-Five

MOTHER RETURNED WITH SOME HERBS. I POUNDED THEM GENTLY on a log with a stick until the leaves became a paste. I unwrapped the blood-soaked fabric from her arm.

The bullet had gone through the middle of her forearm. My stomach lurched. I wanted to look away but forced myself to tear the last sleeve of her shirt, wet it with water, and clean the wound. I put the paste on the wound and wrapped it with the clean fabric.

Nhia's wound was minor. He was lucky a bullet only grazed him. I put paste on his arm and wrapped it while he slept, then did the same for Pa's injuries. Mother lay on the ground next to Nhia and closed her eyes.

Nhia awoke and sobbed weakly. I picked him up, gave him some water, and sat him on my lap. He glanced at the trees and leaned on my chest for support. I kissed his forehead. He was the reason I wasn't insane; he kept my mind off the dead. I'd do anything to keep him safe and bring him to Thailand.

There were no edible plants nearby, and the chattering of morning birds made my stomach rumble more. If I had a bow and arrow or sling shot, we'd have the birds for food. I imagined the smell and taste of the ones Der had baked on the fire in the village. My mouth watered, and I missed my sister.

Mother mumbled in her sleep, "Heaven, help."

I shook her, and she jerked, eyes opening wide.

"What happened?"

"Nightmare." I scooted closer to her and smoothed her hair while fighting my own tears.

Toua returned around noon.

"Sorry, no edible plants," he said. "But I found a place I think is unguarded. We'll rest here until evening."

"How will we cross?" I asked. "I can't swim, and I lost the plastic tube Father gave me. Also, we don't have Nhia's baby carrier to carry him."

Toua grabbed his black backpack, untied the string, and loosened it to open. "Pa's and my tubes are in here. Mother, is yours with you?"

Mother checked the bigger of the two pouches at her waist. "I have it here." The smaller pouch was empty since we'd paid the Laotians with our last silver bar.

"Nou can use mine. I'll swim," said Toua. "I'll tie Nhia onto my back with my rope."

Toua was not a good swimmer, and that worried me. I had heard about people dying as they crossed the river. It would be very risky.

When evening fell, Toua handed Pa a supporting stick. I carried Nhia on my back. We walked slowly toward the Mekong. Darkness crept over the woods as we reached the river. I left Nhia with my mother and walked to the edge. Water babbled below my bare feet and a cold wind brushed my face. The Mekong was wide, and the Thai bank looked far away. I wished for wings.

Toua unpacked his plastic tube and started blowing. Mother handed hers to me. I blew, but the tube didn't get any bigger. My brother grabbed the tube from me and blew hard on it.

"It has a leak. It's useless." He tossed it away.

"How am I going to cross?" Mother's voice rose in panic. "I can't swim, and my arm is hurt."

Toua blew Pa's tube. "This one is bad, too. It probably was punctured when I bumped into a tree. We can't go with just one tube." He threw it on the ground and stamped on it in frustration.

Dread swirled in my stomach. I reached for Mother's hands. "Is there another way?" My voice wobbled.

Silence stretched out between us as we stared at the wide river.

"I'll swim," Toua said. "One of you use the good plastic tube and come with me. Once we're in Thailand, I'll get a canoe and come back."

A canoe? I released a pent-up breath. Separation had never crossed my mind. My brother was braver than me. Father used to say, *"Fearlessness could bring freedom."* Toua was being fearless.

"That will work," I said. "*Tis nyab* and you go. She definitely needs to go tonight. Mother, Nhia, and I will wait here for the canoe."

"I agree," said Mother.

"We'll go then. I'm sorry to leave you three here." Toua clamped a hand on my shoulder. "Nou, be brave. Father once said you have the heart of a man, and I believe him. You lead and take care of Mother and Nhia while I'm gone."

"I'll do my best," I said softly.

I pretended to be brave, but I was terrified.

Pa put the plastic tube around her waist. Toua took a rope from his backpack and tied it around his waist and Pa's to keep them together. They walked slowly down to the river.

I held Mother's good hand as we watched the black figures ease into the water. We lost sight of them in the dark but heard splashing. The splashing grew more frantic, like a wild creature thrashing in the dark water. Mother and I hurried down with

Nhia to the riverbank. Pa was fighting for her life. Toua pulled her back to shore.

"What happened?" Mother demanded.

Pa wheezed. "I sank. I'm too heavy, and I flipped."

"We don't have much time." Toua took Pa's tube from her. "Mother, you come with me."

Mother took the tube but didn't put it on. She gave it to me. "You go with Toua. I'll watch *nyab* and Nhia."

"You go, Mother," I said. "Please, go with him. You need a doctor for your arm as soon as possible."

"I want you to go." Mother spoke slowly and clearly, but I refused to take the tube.

I crossed my arms. "I will not leave without the family."

Mother handed the tube to Toua.

"Use it to get across. We'll wait for you and the canoe."

Toua put the tube on. "Take care of yourself. I'll be back soon."

We sat in the dusky moonlight and watched Toua disappear into the Mekong.

Chapter Twenty-Six

As the night progressed, I paced quietly by the river's edge, watching for signs of a canoe. Cold wind whipped my hair and face. What was taking Toua so long? He had to return before dawn.

Roosters crowed. My heart hammered. Heaven, dawn was breaking and still no canoe. Did Toua reach Thailand? Fear and disappointment frayed my nerves, and with hunger and the cold, my knees gave way. I dragged in big breaths of the cold air. I surveyed the area one more time for a canoe, but there was no sign of Toua. I pushed to my feet and trudged back in the burgeoning dawn light to the others in the trees.

Mother and Pa sat up as I approached. I joined them under the tree.

"No canoe?" Pa asked in a cracked voice.

"Sorry, no canoe," I said softly.

"Do you think he made it to shore?"

"I think he's in Thailand but couldn't find a canoe," said Mother. "We have to move farther back into the trees before the enemy finds us."

"Let's hurry," I said.

I pulled Pa up and gave her the walking stick. I took Nhia from Mother's lap. In the dim light, we picked our way slowly and cautiously to avoid tripping on dead logs and vines.

Bang! Bang! Bang!

We dropped to the ground. My heartbeat roared in my ears. Nhia cried and I clapped a hand over his mouth. The gunshots stopped, and still we remained motionless.

After a long time, we sat up.

Mother whispered, "The guards are awake."

"I-I hope that wasn't Toua coming back," Pa sobbed.

It could be him. My very bones hurt at the thought of Toua dead in the river. How could we go to Thailand without him? What would we do? Who would make decisions? My head throbbed, and I decided that Toua was safe in Thailand. My brother would come for us.

Daylight crawled over the woods. The only sound was the wind in the trees. My stomach growled repeatedly. Was Nhia hungry? His thin, fragile body worried me. A sudden memory of my twin brothers' deaths made me catch my breath.

I couldn't lose Nhia, and I couldn't fail my sister. Closing my eyes, I let out a long, slow breath. I wouldn't allow negative thoughts to drain my energy. I would lead my wounded family to freedom. I would guard them to the best of my physically weak ability.

I untied the canteen on my waist and gulped a mouthful of water. I woke Nhia and gave him some. Mother and Pa finished the canteen. As I tied the canteen back on my waist, the ring hanging on the string hit the canteen, making a tinkling sound.

"Mother, can I have your empty pouch for the ring?" I asked.

Mother gave me the pouch. I handed Nhia to her and tied the pouch around my waist with the ring in it. Three important items were on me: the ring, the machete and the canteen.

Sun rays burst through the thick overgrowth, and the woods grew warmer. Pa moaned softly.

"*Tis nyab*, you're having pain?" I asked.

"Yes." Pa touched her stomach. "I'm afraid I'm going to have the baby."

I threw a worried glance at Mother.

"Let's get ready. We need a sharp piece of fresh, clean bamboo to cut the umbilical cord," said Mother.

"Why can't we use the knife?" I asked.

"Knife is not clean."

My pulse still raced from the gunshots earlier, but I was the only one who was strong enough to get a piece of bamboo. I had no choice. I had to be brave and save my family.

"I'll look for a bamboo grove."

Mother nodded. "You must be careful. If you can't find it, come back. Our last resort is the knife."

I stood and straightened my shoulders. The treetops swayed as gusts of wind swept through the forest. I darted along and stopped often to mark a cross on a tree with my machete. My adrenaline ran high as I searched in vain for edible plants and a bamboo grove. The stories I'd heard about soldiers raping women made my stomach twist in fear. We were so vulnerable.

I found a small trail. I hid behind a tree and watched for signs of people. After a while I followed the trail and came upon a bamboo grove. What a relief! Bamboo stems usually contained water and there could be shoots to eat. But I had to be careful. Stumps and leaves were everywhere. Someone had been in here recently, cutting stalks for thatch huts or a raft.

I browsed quickly for bamboo shoots. There weren't any. I kicked the ground in frustration. I chopped down a bamboo stem and cut each node off for water. There were only a few drops in each node. I sighed heavily. Cold dry season wasn't a good time to travel. I hastily chopped a piece of the stem and followed the trail back.

Mother approved of the bamboo's sharpness. Pa groaned continually, and I

worried someone would hear.

"*Tis nyab*, I know it's painful, but we're in a danger zone," I whispered. "Try not to make noise."

The next contraction, Pa clenched her teeth silently against the pain as she twisted on the ground. I couldn't imagine giving birth. Sweat beaded on my neck as I watched Pa struggle.

"Nou, I want you to look for a log," Mother said, urgently. "*Nyab's* too weak to push."

I scavenged our surrounding area for a log. Focusing on the delivery, I forgot about my hunger. I found a short, thigh-sized log nearby and dragged it over. With all of my strength, I lifted Pa onto the log. I collapsed to the ground, dizzy.

When I heard my name called, I sat up, breathing hard. "What's happened?"

"You fainted." Mother's brow furrowed in worry.

I rose awkwardly to my knees and prayed, "Lord of Heaven, if I am chosen to carry this task, please make the air be my food to give me strength."

I took a few deep breaths and gathered two handfuls of rotten brown leaves and spread them between Pa's legs in case I was unable to catch the baby. Pa sat uncomfortably on the log and tried to hold herself against the tree. She whimpered louder as the contraction deepened.

"My back is killing me," she muttered.

I sat behind Pa, leaning into the rough, hard bark. I wrapped my arms beneath Pa's, making my body a solid cushion for her. She clenched her teeth, twisted her body and grabbed my arms tightly. I tried to hold myself steady against the pain. My body ached and sweat soaked my shirt.

"Push, push harder," Mother said.

With her last bit of energy, Pa pushed as hard as she could. Mother caught the baby just in time with her good hand.

Holding the infant, she grimaced in pain, and I knew her other arm hurt.

"It's a boy," she said proudly.

Despite my fear, I couldn't stop the tears. Pa took off one of her shirts and gave it to Mother as the infant cried.

"Nou, quickly, tie the umbilical cord and cut it," said Mother.

I tied the cord with a piece of string from my torn shirt, reached for the piece of bamboo and pointed it at the belly cord. My hands trembled.

"I won't hurt him," I said under my breath. "I can do it."

I sucked in a breath and sliced the umbilical cord with the sharp bamboo. The infant wailed. Mother gave him to me, and I quickly wrapped him up in Pa's shirt.

On the ground beside me, Nhia looked lifeless. He had slept through the birth.

My arms were bruised. I had no energy left. My body felt like it was filled with wet sand. I longed for my brother. Why wasn't he here?

"I'm so...hungry...thirsty and I have stomach cramps." Pa held her stomach as she lay on the cold ground.

Hunger, dehydration, and blood loss created a deathly pallor on Pa's worn face. Mother massaged Pa's stomach with her good hand.

"The stomach cramp will go away," Mother said. "It happens after birth."

Pa groaned and asked for water. She looked at me with tired, empty eyes. With one arm, I held the baby and reached for the canteen with my other hand. My heart fell. It was empty, and the only canteen we had. Panic rose in my chest, threatening to choke me. I leaned on the tree in an effort to calm myself.

Pa moaned softly and asked again for water. I wanted to scold her. I moved three trees away and still her misery reached me. My headache sharpened, and I closed my eyes. Running away wouldn't solve the problem. A true hero didn't ignore the suffering of others. The heroes in folklore always fought to save lives no matter how dangerous and difficult the situation became. They fought until their last breath. I pictured my heroes, seeing their strength and courage. To help my family, I must put my misery aside. I returned and lay the infant on the ground next to Nhia.

"Mother, I'm going to find water and food."

Mother's tired eyes met mine. "No. You have no strength. Rest so you can take us to the river this evening."

"*Tis nyab* needs water and food before she can walk to the river."

"Who will help you if you fall and can't get up?" Mother asked.

I was afraid of that and everything else, but I tried to smile and said, "I'll be fine. Also, I need to find a good place by the river for us tonight."

Mother threw me a pleading look.

"I'll be fine," I said again. "I will."

"Come back before dark, so we have time to get down to the river."

I nodded, then tied the canteen, machete, and the waist pouch to my pants. I had to go do my best, or I'd regret it forever. I took a deep breath and set out to find food and water.

Chapter Twenty-Seven

I VENTURED TOWARD THE RIVER. THE COLD AIR GRADUALLY DRIED my sweat. I was relieved the birthing was done. My next challenge was to keep my family alive and get them to Thailand.

Hunger and thirst sapped my strength. I sat down to rest and scanned the treetops. A bird sat on a near branch. I eyed it wistfully, imagining its tender flesh cooked over a fire. My mouth watered.

The bird flew to the tree I leaned against. It reminded me of the folk tale of *Txiv Laus Luam Mus Tua Cuam*. In the story, a bird saved Yer, the main character. My desire to eat the bird shifted. I got on my knees and bowed beneath the tree.

"Bird, please fly to Thailand and tell General Vang Pao that my family needs help. Please, please go tell him to send help as soon as possible."

The bird flew away. I imagined it flying to the General's home and talking to him. He was sending help. I grasped the tree and slowly pulled myself to my feet. I headed to the Mekong River, hoping to find the place where Toua had left us the night before. With luck, I'd find water, too, and maybe something to eat.

As I neared the river, I knelt behind some trees and watched for enemy guards who might patrol the area. No one was around. I advanced slowly. Suddenly, a heavy footstep cracked a twig. Leaves rustled. Fear stole my breath. The sound drew closer. I peered through the trees. Two guards in dark green uniforms walked along the riverbank. If that twig hadn't cracked, I'd have been caught. I curled up into a ball underneath the tree. My legs shook, and I tried to slow my breath. I prayed to my father, my ancestors, and the Lord of Heaven.

I waited until the footsteps faded, then waited some more. When all was quiet, I slowly uncoiled. I wanted to quit my search, but my heroes didn't quit when faced with danger. To be a hero, I couldn't allow fear to take over. I inspected the area and edged closer to the riverbank, listening and watching. There were no wells, no edible plants. I looked for the place Toua had told us to wait.

Not too far along, I found an area of crushed leaves. The trees seemed like the ones we had leaned on last night. I would bring my family here to wait for Toua. I stepped cautiously down to the river's edge. A medium height tree with low drooping branches and roots sticking out of the ground stood on the shore. I stood tall by it, looking at the distant line of trees on the other side of the Mekong River. The trees belonged to the Thai. I studied the wide river.

"Why can't I swim, and why are you so big, Mother River?" I asked.

Mountain ranges to the west half covered the sun. It would be dark soon. I had no clean water and food to bring back to the family. The Mekong was muddy brown, filled with trash and dead people. The villagers bathed and washed clothes in it, too. I wouldn't drink the Mekong's filthy water.

I staggered toward the woods. My throat was so dry, and exhaustion weighed me down. After a few more steps, I fell to the brown dirt on the riverbank. Dizziness took me, and my heart pounded heavily. I lay still for a while.

A voice whispered in my head. "Drink the Mekong water. It will give you strength."

I stared at the river and muttered, "If you were me, would you drink the filthy water?"

But I had no choice. I crawled to the river. I closed my eyes, so I wouldn't see the muddy brown water and imagined myself swallowing fresh, clean water. I cupped my hands together and scooped water into my mouth. I drank until I was satisfied and filled the canteen. Energy filled me.

MOTHER SAT BACK WITH A DEEP SIGH WHEN SHE CAUGHT SIGHT of me returning. Her hollowed cheeks and the dark circles under her eyes made her look as old as my grandmother. A month had changed her appearance drastically.

"I was so worried about you," she said.

"Sorry."

I handed Pa the canteen.

"You found fresh water?" Pa asked and took it.

"It's from the Mekong."

"That's polluted water." Her eyes narrowed. "My father was a nurse during the war, and he said dirty things have germs and bacteria that could make a person sick. I'm already weak. I can't get sick."

"You're right." I took back the canteen. "None of you should drink this filthy water. You are all vulnerable to illness."

I wished I hadn't drunk so much of it. Heaven, I couldn't get sick. My family needed me. Mother must have read my expression.

"You'll be all right," she said. "You are healthy."

If I had a pot, I'd boil the water. If I went back to the field, I might be able to trace my lost basket, and other people's supplies, too. Unless the Communists took them.

The new baby's fussing stirred me. I picked him up from the ground and rewrapped him tighter to keep him warm. One cry could get us all killed, but I wouldn't give him opium. He could die from the drug.

"*Tis nyab,* have you picked a name for him yet?" I asked.

"I'm still thinking about it."

"I think we should name him TouZou (*Tub Zoov*) since he's a son born in the forest. What do you think?" I asked.

"It's a good name," she said.

"I like it," Mother whispered. "Son of the jungle."

"Your name will be TouZou," I whispered. "We'll do a soul-calling for you when we get to Thailand."

Dusk approached. It was time. I couldn't carry two children without a baby carrier. I had no strength. I was angry at Toua. Why hadn't he returned? Was he dead? How could we cross without him?

"Mother and *tis nyab,* I'll have to do two trips. Which one of you want to go first with a child?"

"One trip," Mother said. "I'll carry TouZou with my good arm."

"But you don't have strength," I said. "You'll fall."

"I can do it. I can always rest if I need to."

"I can help Mother carry TouZou," Pa murmured.

I found a walking stick for Pa and carried Nhia.

"Tonight is our chance," Mother said, with TouZou on her arm. "I think Toua will be back."

She still believed he was alive. I hoped she was right.

"Everything will be all right tonight." Pa sounded confident.

"I can feel Father's spirit guiding me," I said. "If I pray to him, I won't be discouraged and afraid."

We walked as slow as turtles. Pa and Mother grimaced with pain but didn't complain. Night had nearly fallen by the time we reached the river. We rested under a tree by the shore in the same spot we waited the night before.

"Mother, it's warmer here, so you all stay in this spot," I said.

"Where are you going?"

"If I can climb that tree," I pointed my finger at a dark shape a little further south on the riverbank, "I'll have a better view of any canoe coming our way."

"You don't need to climb a tree," Mother whispered.

"A canoeist won't see us here in the dark. If I am in the tree, my whistle will be heard further away. The man will see the tree and know where the noise comes from."

"How will you know whether the canoe is Toua's or the enemy's?" Pa's voice was edged with fear. "The enemy patrols the river with their canoes."

She was right. I wouldn't know whose canoe it was out there. "If there is a canoe, it could be Toua, the Thai, or the Communist Pathet Lao. We had to take the risk. I think we'll be all right."

Mother grasped my hands. "We'll wait here for you. Ger told us that there are Thai peasants who take in refugees for money. There's hope for a canoe."

I nodded in the dark and walked away. The air was cold, but so far, no wind gusts like the first night. I studied the tree. Then I took a quick, short jump and grabbed hold of a branch. I was unable to lift myself and hung like a monkey. I gathered all my strength and got my feet up on the trunk but lost strength and fell on my back. The air whooped out of me, and my bones felt shattered.

"Are you all right?" Mother hurried to my side, short of breath.

She pulled me to sit up with her good arm. I straightened my shoulders and stretched both arms. I felt no pain, except for my back.

"Don't hurt yourself," she cried. "Please, don't climb the tree."

"I have to. The canoeist must hear me. I should be able to climb this small tree." I took a breath. "It seems easy when Toua climbs a tree as short as this."

"You're as clever and capable as any man. You're just too weak. Don't compare yourself to Toua or your father." My mother brushed my hair back. "You're a very brave daughter. That's why we've come this far."

No matter how difficult, I had to fight for our lives. I scrambled to my feet gracelessly. "I'm not giving up."

"I'll help you." Mother moved closer to the tree trunk. "Get on my shoulders."

"No. Don't hurt your arm more."

"I'll use my back. You jump and grab the second branch. Put your feet on my back, and I'll push you up as I stand."

It could work. I jumped and my feet hung above the ground. Mother crouched and I put my feet on her back. She slowly rose, and I was able to swing my legs onto the branch.

"Are you all right up there?" asked Mother breathlessly.

"I'm fine," I said, but my breathing was shallow. "Be careful as you go back."

I sat with my right side against the tree trunk and my feet resting on the branch below. I focused on the wide river and the dim lights on the Thai shore. When the lights were extinguished and the world was in complete darkness, I knew it must be close to midnight. My body ached.

As I turned to change my position, gunshots rumbled from the south. My heart fluttered and my nerves lurched with each sound. I hugged the branch to keep from falling. People must be trying to cross. The shooting might frighten Toua if he was trying to cross or any Thai who might be trolling for refugees. Why was everything going wrong?

A voice in my head said, "Be strong. Don't give up hope."

I bit my lip to stop it from trembling.

When all was quiet, my muscles relaxed, and I breathed more deeply. My legs cramped from being in the tree for so long. If Father was with us, would we be in Thailand now? His spirit was guiding me, giving me courage. Was that his voice in my head? It sounded like him. I needed him. I didn't want to believe I was out of my mind or so desperate to survive that I invented his presence.

"Father, what should I do next if there's no canoe tonight?" I murmured. "Your dream of having grandchildren to carry on the family name came true when TouZou was born. Now help me save him and Nhia. Guide me."

I'd do anything to save my family, but I couldn't control our destiny. I counted my family members. When the twins were born, the family grew. Pa, TouZou and Nhia were new additions. Including Grandmother and the new additions, there had been eleven. Now, only five remained. If we didn't get to Thailand soon, the family would disappear like the white dust that scattered in the air. No one would know where we had existed.

The dark river gurgled. No sign of a canoe. Gazing at the night sky, I murmured, "Where are the Americans who promised to take care of the Hmong whether they won or lost the Secret War?"

The Americans got the Hmong involved in the war, and when they were losing, they left us to suffer on our own. If not for the Americans giving the Hmong the idea of democracy, the Communists would have left us alone. They wouldn't have searched for former CIA soldiers to slaughter, and Father wouldn't have lived in fear of being caught. He wouldn't have been murdered by the communists. We wouldn't have been forced to flee and wouldn't be waiting so desperately for rescue.

I wanted to scream as loud as thunder at the world, the war, and the pain in my cramped legs. If I ever made it to Thailand and to America and learned to read and write, I'd write the story of this grief. Every day, misery seared a huge wound deep inside my heart. No one could see the wound, but the pain would remain with me forever.

Roosters crowed. Still no canoe. What happened to Toua? He wouldn't abandon us, and I refused to believe he was dead. The break of dawn could mean the end of our lives. Without food and energy, we might not survive another day.

"Father," I whispered. "I tried. I watched the river the whole night. There's nothing I can do now."

"Don't ever give up," the voice said. *"You can do more."*

What else could I do?

Chapter Twenty-Eight

SOFT DAYLIGHT APPROACHED. THE FAMILY RETREATED BACK TO the woods.

TouZou was awake and fussy. Pa fed him. He was unsatisfied and flailed his arms and made unhappy noises. I refused to use opium to quiet him. I picked him up and rocked him back and forth. Pa sobbed quietly.

"What's wrong?" I asked.

"I'm so sorry," she said between tears. "My son and I are a burden for you."

"Not at all." I kept my voice low. "I wish I had more strength, so I could do more."

I rewrapped the infant and rocked him some more. He fell asleep, and I rested underneath a tree with him. I had no more energy. My eyes grew heavy, and my brain shut down. My worries, pain and fear, and exhaustion pinned me to the ground. I lay with the child on my arms.

Nhia's cry woke me.

"Water, water," Nhia cried softly.

Mother comforted him, but he wouldn't stop. My heart

throbbed for my failure to get water for my family. Heaven, help me. Where could I get clean water and food?

I stared at the trees. What would Father do? He risked his life taking the family from Phou Bia Mountain to the village. What would a hero do? In the folk tales, the heroes used their skills.

The orphan boy built a raft. I knew how to build, and there was a bamboo grove. I could build a raft. Inspiration filled me, and strength surged. The nap had helped to clear my head and exhaustion.

A raft. It would take time and strength to build it correctly. My family needed food and water right now. A thought occurred to me. I could go back to the field. If our things were still there, I could use a pot to boil the filthy Mekong water. If they were gone, I'd travel to the village.

Being a girl, I wouldn't be a threat to the villagers. My Lao language skills would help me communicate. Though I wasn't fluent, they would understand me. If worse came to worst, I'd beg and hope they'd spare my life. It would be risky, but what else could I do?

I breathed deeply and decided to try the fields first. *Fearlessness could bring freedom.* If I died, at least it was for my family.

The sun rose high.

"Mother, I'm going to look for food." I left before she had a chance to respond, staggering a bit as I headed toward the fields.

I came upon a rice paddy field that had been harvested. A girl about ten years old was in the field with a small bamboo basket in her hand, chasing insects. I watched the girl from behind a big tree. She seemed harmless, and she could probably get me food and water. But she might tell her parents. What if her father came to the woods and searched for my family and killed us all? What if he raped us? My heart beat fast.

Every decision carried a risk. Doing nothing had its own risk. Actions had consequences. The heroes in the stories embraced their decisions and weren't scared of bad outcomes. I took deep breaths and decided to approach her.

"Sister," I called in Lao.

The girl looked in my direction. I approached as she stared. I tried my best to

speak Lao. "My son is starving. He needs food. Can you help me save him?"

"How old is he?" she asked.

I showed three fingers.

"We don't have food." Her brown eyes surveyed the brown rice plant stumps.

"Please. My son will die if he doesn't get water and food soon. I beg you," I said.

"My family is poor."

I took Der's beautiful silver ring out from the pouch and showed it to her. The girl's eyes lit up.

"If you bring me rice and water, I'll give you this ring," I said.

The girl nodded. "I need your canteen for the water."

"Clean the canteen before filling it." I wanted to make sure no Mekong germs remained, so I demonstrated and gave the canteen to her. "Quickly. My son is waiting. We don't need your parents' help, so don't mention this to them."

The girl left. I went back to hide behind the trees.

A little while later, she returned alone with sticky rice wrapped in a banana leaf. The canteen was filled with water. I smiled and gave her the ring.

"Thank you so much." I wanted to cry tears of joy.

"I hope your son gets better," she said.

"He'll be happy you helped save him. Again, don't mention this to your parents. Your help was all we needed."

The girl nodded and walked down the path she came from. I trudged off a different path, trying to hide my direction. In the dense woods, I stopped, gulped a mouthful of water, and ate a little bit of the rice. For a moment, a lightness overcame my limbs, then strength began to seep into my body. I hurried back to the hideout, hoping the girl wouldn't tell her parents. I showed the rice to Mother and Pa.

"Did you steal the food?" Mother asked, wide-eyed.

"No. I bought it with Der's ring."

Mother's lips quirked into a smile.

Pa sat up. Her eyes gleamed. "Give me some."

My family's brief happiness heartened my spirit. The sticky rice was about the size of my two fists together. Everyone had a share. I felt stronger now and ready to move into my next plan.

"Mother, we don't know if Toua will ever come. I want to make a raft."

Her eyes shimmered with moisture. "You are right, my clever daughter. Do you know how to build one?"

"In one of Aunty Shoua's stories, the orphan boy made a raft by putting the bamboo stems together and tying them with thin bamboo strips. I built fences and helped Father and Toua with one of our houses. I think I can make one."

Hope lit Mother's face. "Excellent. I can help."

Help would be good, but Mother could barely walk and had to avoid hurting her injured arm.

"The children and *tis nyab* need you. You stay with them. I'll be back soon," I told her.

At the grove, I used the machete to chop down a few bamboo stems. I split a stem in half and cut it into four lengths. Then, I cut the lengths into very thin strips. The physical work drained every bit of my strength. There was no way I could make a sturdy raft big enough to fit five people. What could I do?

I rested, steadying my thoughts. The only thing I came up

with was I had to go alone to Thailand to get help. It was the best way. Maybe the only way. But how could I leave my family? Anything could happen to them or me while we were apart. If something happened to me, what would become of them? As I listened to my head and heart, it all came down to do something or die. I decided to go to Thailand alone.

I lined up three short stems on the ground, parallel to each other. I put six long stems on top of the shorter ones. I tied the stems together with the bamboo strips, checking to ensure each intersection was tied tightly. Then I tied four small bamboo poles on the raft, one on each side, so I had something to grab or hold on to if I slipped off.

The raft felt sturdy enough. I split the medium-sized bamboo stem in half, about an arm's length, and shaped it into a paddle. Pride filled me as I looked over my work. I took the raft to the river and hid it in the shrubs.

I had put all my energy into the raft. If it didn't work or the plan didn't go well, I didn't know what else to do.

At the hideout, I told my family about the raft and my plan.

"Although you are born a girl, you are truly a son to me," Mother said with pride. "When I was young, I was told that girls are timid and weak. In my lifetime, I've not seen a girl as brave and capable as you are. Nou, I'm so lucky you are mine. You are my indispensable daughter."

My heart warmed and I believed I could do anything. "Thank you, Mother. Your kind words give me courage. I am an ordinary girl. I just have no choices."

"Nou, you are a bold girl," Pa said. "I admire you. I wouldn't have done what you did. Thank you for doing everything to save our lives."

"I hope I can get help to bring everyone to Thailand," I said.

"Any hope we have is because of you," Pa said. "You won't abandon us."

"As long as I live, I will not." I gave the machete to Mother. "Keep this safe. I don't want to lose it in the water."

I wanted her to have the knife because if I didn't return, they would need it to survive.

Chapter Twenty-Nine

I REACHED THE MEKONG JUST AS DARK FELL. I CARRIED THE family's prayers and hoped our ancestors would protect my crossing and my family until I returned. Quickly, I uncovered the raft and, the bamboo paddle in hand, pulled the raft to the river. The dim light on the Thai shore provided direction. Like the orphan in the story, I slipped my raft into the shallow water and stepped into the cold Mekong River. I had no strength to stand on the raft like the orphan boy did. Sitting was the wisest option. I sat and curled one leg under me on the raft and steadied myself with the other leg in the water.

My weight made the raft wobble. I steadied it with my leg and the paddle. Heaven, if I slipped off it, I'd disappear beneath the murky water. My stomach churned. I released a deep breath and moved slowly into deeper water. I pulled my leg up onto the raft and started paddling.

The flowing water pushed me south. I prayed, "Father, grandparents, and my ancestors, please help me. Help me move the raft straight. I must go straight so I can find my family later. Protect me and bring a canoe to me. Please, please."

I paddled toward the light, faith in my ancestors giving me

strength. The chilly winds gave me goosebumps, and the cold water that leaked onto the raft numbed my feet and legs. The water frightened me and so did the prospect of meeting Pathet Lao guards. But my family's lives depended on me, so I ignored my fear and paddled faster. The shakier I felt, the faster I paddled.

My lungs burned with each stroke and deep, sharp pain pierced my elbows and arms. It hurt like hell, but a hero would never give up. I had to be my family's hero.

Midway across the river, I spotted a dark shape closer to the Thai shore. I looked carefully. I couldn't believe what I was seeing. It was a canoe! A surge of hope washed over me. The heaviness in my chest lifted, and I paddled quickly toward the canoe.

As my raft neared the canoe, I called out softly in Lao, "Help, help."

The canoe sailed toward me. Soon it reached me, and I discerned two men.

"You coming alone?" asked a man in Lao.

"More people are waiting on the other side," I said, panting. "Take me with you. I will take you to them."

"Do you have money?"

"Yes," I lied. "My mother has it."

One of the men pulled me to their canoe. I sat in the middle, catching my breath, while the men paddled toward the Lao shore. As the men talked, I smelled alcohol. I hoped they were good people.

"How long have you been there?" one man asked.

"Three nights," I said. "I looked for a canoe but didn't find one."

"We were out here last night but saw no indication of any refugee people," he replied.

If I hadn't paddled over, we might have died there. We reached the Lao shore, and I took them to the hideout. Mother and Pa squealed with delight. This was the first moment of happiness we had experienced in longer than I could remember. A moment of accomplishment that empowered me.

"Thank our ancestors, you are back," cried Mother.

One of the men shined a flashlight at Mother.

"We want money now," he demanded.

Pa drew a deep, shuddering breath. Mother looked down, unable to speak.

"We'll give you opium now," I said quickly. "And money when we get to Thailand."

Even if I had money, I wouldn't pay them now. The other guides had taught us valuable lessons. Mother gave me the machete and the men the last opium dosage, the size of my thumb. The men were satisfied and helped the children, Mother, and Pa to the canoe. We all squeezed into the center of the canoe. As we sailed away from the Lao shore, tears welled up behind my eyes. Safety, for the first time, was in reach.

But we still had a large challenge ahead. The smell of alcohol on their breaths worried me, though. What would they do when they found out we had no money? Maybe they would rape us. If worse came to worst, I'd use the machete to kill them. It was a relief to have the knife, but I didn't have much strength. On impulse, I took the paper out of the machete and put it in the pouch.

We reached the Thai shore at dawn. I held Nhia and whispered to him, "We are in Thailand. If your father has not gone to America, he is here somewhere."

Nhia murmured something I couldn't understand. We got out of the canoe and sat on the sand.

"Where's the money?" one man asked.

"The guides took all our money," I said. "Take us to our relatives in the camp. They have money. We'll pay you."

"You lied to us!" the man yelled.

He slapped my face so hard, warm blood dripped down the

side of my mouth. Nhia cried softly. That was the loudest noise he'd made in a long time. I bit back my pain and anger. The man kicked sand, and it flew everywhere. I lowered my head to cover Nhia's face from getting the dirt in his eyes. He shook with fear.

"Search them!" he shouted.

One man searched Mother while the other searched me. He untied the pouch, the canteen, and the machete and threw them on the sand. I bit back tears. With his flashlight, he searched the pouch, took out the rolled paper, looked at it with no interest, and threw it at me. I breathed in relief.

He roughly searched me in an effort to find any jewelry sewn in my ragged, stained clothes. After he found nothing, he kicked more sand and took the canteen and the machete.

"Please give the knife back," I begged, trying to boost my volume with all the breath I had. "It belongs to my father and it's the only memory of him. He was killed during the journey."

"If you want the knife, find money."

"I will. Take us to our relatives. I beg you."

"These women have nothing," said the other man. "What do we do with them?"

"Take them back to Laos!" the other growled.

My stomach clenched as hard as a stone. "Please, I beg you, don't take us back. They'll kill us. We lost everything. We have nothing but our souls. We will find money. I promise."

He grunted angrily, and my heart pounded.

"You see, my mother was shot on her arm. You can't send us back," I pleaded.

He shone his flashlight on Mother, who sat on the sand crying. He walked to her and looked at her wounded arm.

"All right," he said. "We'll give you time to find your people."

A pent-up breath escaped my lips. "Thank you. Can you take us to the refugee camp?"

The man pointed to a home in the distance. "The couple in

the house takes care of the refugees after they are dropped off. They know where the refugees are taken. I'll go talk to them when they are up."

The sky began to lighten. My gratitude toward our rescuers disappeared. They were evil. I couldn't look at them directly. I studied them from the corner of my eye. One was younger, tall and slim, about thirty. The other was about forty, short and muscular. They both had dark skin, which reminded me of the Laotian escorts who had abandoned us.

Standing tall by their canoe, the men watched us as if we were prisoners. The younger one stared at me. I kept my head low and held Nhia close to my face to conceal it from the man. We hadn't bathed since we had left our village, and I was sure we looked disgusting and smelled unpleasant. Even though the men left us alone, not touching us, I still worried they would paddle us back to Laos if we didn't find money. I longed for Toua.

The older man set off toward the house with the tamarind and mango trees. The younger one stayed and stared. The area had a beautiful view of the Mekong River. Far away on the other side were the woods where we'd hidden. I would hate to return.

A while later, two new men approached. One was young like Toua, the other old. They seemed like Hmong, but I couldn't be sure.

They reached us and the old man said, "You made it."

He spoke Hmong! Happiness and hope flared inside of me.

Color flooded Mother's sunken cheeks. "You are Hmong," she sobbed. "Help us. The Thai men will take us back if we don't pay them. We have no money."

"Don't worry," the man replied. "They told me about you, and I paid them a silver bar. You can pay me back when you have the money."

Unbelievable! My spirits lifted. "Thank you." I mustered a smile. "You saved us."

The young man's eyes were on me. "You're welcome." His deep, husky voice made my heart flutter. "What's your name?" he asked.

Shy, I lowered my head. "Nou Vang."

"My name is Kou Xiong. This is my father, Chong Doua."

I glanced at them. Kou had an oval face and was thin and handsome. He was taller than his father, who had a round face with saggy eyelids and wrinkles creasing his forehead.

"Thank you for saving our lives, Chong Doua," said Mother.

He smiled. "I'm glad I can help. We're here to take you inside. My family got here at midnight, so we're also new."

Mother managed a half-smile. "Again, thank you."

"Uncle Chong Doua," I said, shyly. "I know we are asking a lot, but my mother was shot on the arm. The bleeding stopped but she needs to see a doctor before it gets bad. Can you help?"

He checked Mother's arm. "She needs to go to the hospital. I'll take her."

"Can I go, too?" I asked.

"We'll see."

The older Thai man who had my knife returned.

"Can I have my knife back?" I asked.

"No," he said. "It's mine now."

"You said if we give you money, you'd give it back."

"I lied to you just like you lied to me."

The man smirked. I had no power to get it back. Rage made me forget my fear, and I screamed, scaring Nhia who gripped my arm and wept.

"I'll pay for the knife," said Kou in Lao. "How much is it?"

I eyed Kou in shock. What a kind man. His act of kindness meant the world to me.

The Thai man studied the machete. "A silver bar."

Chong Doua shook his head. "It's not worth that much. We can use the money to take your mother to the hospital."

"I don't have a silver bar," Kou said. "Can you lower the price?"

The Thai man shook his head and faced me. "Your father's precious weapon is now mine."

I made a fist in readiness to curse him but gulped down my words. He might still try to drag us back across the river. I wouldn't allow my anger and frustration to cost my family their safety. Thank goodness I had taken my father's document out of the machete. At least I had that.

"Sorry, I was unable to help you," Kou said in a low voice.

"It's all right," I said. "I appreciate your help. Thank you."

Chapter Thirty

My family followed Kou and Uncle to a wooden house on stilts with a corrugated aluminum roof. Taking the small, short staircase was like climbing a steep hill. We stopped to catch our breaths after each step. Kou supported Mother and took his time to make sure we didn't fall and hurt ourselves.

The owners of the house, a man and woman in their sixties, greeted us and introduced themselves. The man's name was Aran, and his wife was Isra. They spoke with us for a long time, but their language was Thai, and their unfamiliar words flew over my head like the wind.

Isra brought a bamboo bucket the size of a melon that was half-full of sticky rice, some salt, and water. My mouth watered and my stomach rumbled. I dipped rice in the salt and fed Nhia. He ate so slowly that I couldn't wait, and I ate while feeding him. Mother and Pa ate small portions. TouZou fussed at his mother's breast. Pa had little milk for him, but I was optimistic that with some nourishment, she'd have milk in the coming days.

On the wooden floor lay Chong Doua's wife and two boys. She was awake, but the children snored like they had no fear.

They probably had nothing to worry about because they had their parents. They had no idea what my family had gone through.

"Call me Aunt Chong Doua," said the woman. "What's your name?"

"Nou Vang. When did you get here?" I asked.

"Midnight. Did you have problems crossing the river?"

Mother nodded and sadness appeared in her eyes. "It has been a long, tragic journey."

"I'm sorry to hear that. We were very lucky there was no killing."

Aunt Chong Doua told us how her family came from Phua Houa village, and they had traveled alone safely. Uncle Chong Doua was a resistance fighter and had come to Thailand once by himself in 1975 when the Communists took power in Laos. He was familiar with the geography and knew which area were safe to cross. Mother recounted our story. We wept with her as she described all that had happened.

Isra came back from the store with some baby milk and a bottle for TouZou. She gave him his first bath and provided the two families with sticky rice and a plate of fried fish for a late breakfast. My family got to eat twice, and life began to seep back into me. I couldn't believe our good fortune. The Thai couple's generosity gave me hope.

After breakfast, Uncle and the Thai man, Aran, left on an errand. I wondered when Uncle could arrange for my mother to see a doctor. I hoped he'd do it soon before I nagged him. Aunt refused my help cleaning up, and I appreciated her letting me rest and tend to Nhia.

When Aunt took her rest, I said, "This Thai couple is so kind."

"They're a good couple, but we paid them a silver bar to take our family in last night. If we weren't here, you'd have to pay them."

My head jerked back. "Did you pay her to buy the baby formula, too?"

"No. But a silver bar is worth about 3,000 Thai bahts. That was why she bought the formula."

We owed the Xiong family a great deal.

Suddenly, Nhia sat up on my lap without support. Food was magic.

He looked at everyone and cried softly, "Mom. Mom."

Broken-hearted, I held him tight. Memory of my sister's death overcame me, and I couldn't stop the tears. My chest heaved and sobs caught in my throat.

"I want my mom." Nhia looked around the room.

When he didn't see his mother, he clung to me and cried. I was relieved he was fully conscious. He loved me, but I wasn't his mother. I gazed at my mother for help. She extended her arms to take Nhia, but he pushed her off. I rocked him back and forth as he cried. Kou reached out to Nhia, but that only made him cry harder. Everyone watched helplessly. Stories had helped him before, and the owl story was his favorite.

"Owl, owl," I said. "I'll tell you the story if you stop crying."

He slowly stopped sobbing, but tears continued to slide down his cheeks. I set him on the mat beside me. With my hands held over my head as antlers, I was the deer, calling and looking for my pack. Then I changed to the owl with wide eyes.

"Deer, come over here! There are lots of nuts over by me!"

The deer ran to the owl only to see the owl's big, round, scary eyes. There were no nuts. The frightened deer rushed away and tripped on a pumpkin. The pumpkin rolled and hit the sesame plant hard. I acted out each part as best as I could and used expression. Kou and his brothers watched me with sparkling eyes. When I finished the story, I was out of breath.

"Impressive!" Kou said. "You are a good storyteller. Who taught you stories?"

I blushed. "My parents, Grandmother, and Aunty Shoua, a very good storyteller who lived in my village."

"I love your story," ten-year-old Xao said. "Tell us another one."

"When I have more strength and more breath."

Mother smiled. "I was wrong about stories being useless. On this journey, I saw how stories entertain our mind and relieve our stress."

I tucked that away to hold close. Mother finally saw the value of stories. Nhia fell asleep. Exhausted, I slept with him on the mat.

I woke with a shudder, my heart thumping violently. Another loud gunshot sounded near the house. Quickly, I picked up Nhia and rushed to the Thai couple's bedroom.

"Don't worry," Aunt said. "It's not the Pathet Lao." She smiled, but the sound terrified me.

"What is it?" I asked.

"It's the sound of a car engine. Go check it out. It must have stopped near the house."

Xao and thirteen-year-old Xeng looked at me as if I was mad. When I didn't see Kou, I was glad. I didn't want him to think I was a scaredy-cat. I carried Nhia down the stairs. Mother sat on the lower step.

"Mother, what was the noise?" I asked.

"A car stopped here."

The sun was high. A black, rustic car sat parked on the dirt road. A man chatted with Aran, Uncle, and Kou. Nhia clung tightly to me as Kou walked toward us.

Kou's lips curved upward as he reached us. "Nou, you look livelier after your nap."

I was embarrassed for taking a nap, but it was the first real sleep I'd had in weeks.

"This car will take your mother to the hospital." He looked at Mother. "Are you ready?"

She nodded. "Yes. Thank you for arranging it."

"You're welcome." Kou turned to me. "Would Nhia be all right staying with your sister-in-law?"

"No," I said. "Can I take him along?"

Kou bit his lip. "The hospital is full of sick people. You don't want him to get sick. You should stay with him. My father and I will go with your mother."

"You are taking my mother?" I asked in surprise.

"Yes. I planned to take you and her, but you must stay here, so my father will go along."

I didn't want Mother to be a burden to anyone, but I couldn't risk Nhia getting sick.

"That's very kind of you," I said. "Thank you."

"Don't worry about me," Mother said. "Take good care of yourself, your sister-in-law, and your nephews."

I nodded. "Don't be scared. You have Kou and Uncle with you."

Mother smiled at Kou. "You have a kind, big heart."

"Thank you, Aunty." Kou looked at me in amusement. "Nou, I see that you are the young guardian of your family. Try not to worry about your mother."

I laughed softly, unbelieving that a stranger saw me as the guardian. Maybe my love and care for my family qualified me. I'd take it. "You are observant."

"It's obvious," said Kou. "I'll try my best to take good care of your mother. I'll stay with her."

Gratitude burst inside me, and I couldn't stop my tears.

"Don't cry," said Kou. He edged closer.

He was tall. I tilted my head up to meet his eyes. My body tensed. It felt awkward but also good. I had never experienced such a feeling. Nhia cried. I took a step back and hushed Nhia.

"Your help means so much to me." I wiped my eyes with the back of my hand.

His face lit. "I'm glad you accept my help because you have a lot on your plate. You don't have to take care of them alone."

What a gentleman! A weight lifted from my spirit. I couldn't help but smile.

"You need to smile more." Kou turned to Mother. "I'll help you to the car."

I watched Mother, Kou, Uncle, and Aran get in the car. Then the car took them away.

EVENING ARRIVED. MOTHER, UNCLE, KOU, AND ARAN HADN'T returned, and Isra explained to us that they had to spend the night in the hospital due to Mother's severe arm injury.

That night, I had my first bath in over a month, with shampoo and a bar of soap that smelled like sweet herbs. I went to bed feeling so much better, clean, and refreshed. Still, I tossed and turned thinking about my mother and brother. Mother had been having nightmares and, although Kou said he would take care of her, I still worried because she needed me to comfort her. Toua was always on my mind. What had happened to my brother?

It was close to noon the following day when Mother returned. Her arm was amputated at the elbow and wrapped in white cloth. I cried for her missing hand.

"Don't cry," Mother said. "I no longer have two hands, but the doctor got rid of my pain. I am better now." She handed me a plastic bag that contained bandages, gauzes, ointments, alcohol, and other things for her arm. "In a few days, we'll clean my arm and put new dressing on."

"Your mother is brave like you." Kou's expression was very serious. "She tolerated her pain well. She had a nightmare when we were there, so the doctor gave her some medications to help her."

"Thanks for everything." I turned to Uncle. "Uncle Chong Doua, how much do I owe you?"

"The cost of the doctor and hospital is free since we are refugees. I paid for the rides to and from the hospital and food but not a lot."

"My family will pay you back someday," I promised.

"Take your time," he said.

Uncle went to the stairs and said loudly, "Everyone, get ready. When the *songthaew* taxi gets here, we're going to the refugee camp."

Xao said, "Finally. We've been waiting for so long."

I knew we were a burden to the Xiong family. Without us, they'd have gone to the camp yesterday morning.

Isra returned from her errand. She gave Pa, Mother, and me each a used skirt and shirt to replace our ragged, dirty, and blood-stained clothes. The flowery knee-length skirt was big for my slim body, so I tied it with my sash to keep it from falling off. I felt naked with my legs showing, but I had to get used to it. Nhia and I walked slowly around the house waiting for the taxi.

Kou came toward us with a dazzling smile. "You are beautiful in your new clothes."

He stopped an arm's length from us and studied me. I blushed. Nhia cried, and I picked him up. He buried his face against my shoulder. Kou watched and wouldn't stop smiling. His white, even teeth made him even more attractive. Butterflies skittered across the insides of my stomach. Sucking a breath, I reminded myself that I had promised Mother not to get married, so I must not allow myself to give in to temptation.

"I'm sorry about the tragedy you and your family went through." The concern in Kou's voice touched me. "Your mother told me a lot about you. I was shocked to learn you made a raft and sailed to Thailand. That was bold of a girl your age. How did you find the courage?"

My mother's bragging embarrassed me. "When you face danger, you have to fight for your life." I released a breath. "Now that I think about it, I can't believe I did it."

Kou's eyes twinkled. "You are incredible. Not everyone has such courage. My brother Xeng is thirteen and he couldn't go pee by himself during our journey. He wouldn't survive alone in the woods."

His words made me feel special, but I couldn't face another trek like that. I hoped it was my first and last.

"Kou, I can't thank you and your family enough for saving us. I prayed a lot. Maybe my family was destined to meet yours."

"I'm glad you feel that way." He shrugged. "I haven't done much."

"Your mother said you are eighteen, but you seem mature for your age."

"Mature?" he laughed. "My parents scold me for my lack of skills."

"Are you the oldest?" I asked.

"No. I have two older brothers and two older sisters who are married and gone to America. I'm the middle, middle child."

"Me too." My chest tightened. "Except my siblings are dead. Well, I think one is missing."

His expression clouded. "I'm so sorry."

The taxi arrived, and Uncle called everyone to come out. The songthaew taxi was twice the size of a car. It had four wheels, two seats at the front, and two rows of bench seats on the truck bed, which had a roof.

We thanked Aran and Isra and said goodbye to them. Everyone got in the taxi. Yellow dust flew over us as the taxi bumped down the dirt road. When we reached the highway, fresh air filled the taxi from the open back. Trees, fields, and houses stretched as far as the eye could see.

The motion of the car made me feel odd. My surroundings blurred. My head spun and nausea washed over me. With Nhia on one arm, I grabbed the garbage can in the corner just in time. Everyone except my nephews, Uncle, and Kou vomited. Earlier, I couldn't wait for my first ride and thought it would be amazing, but it wasn't. Why was riding in a car so horrible? Now the taxi smelled of rotting fish from the fish sauce in the papaya salad we ate for lunch. I was too exhausted to care. Thankfully Nhia slept through the turmoil. I leaned against the side of the taxi and closed my eyes.

Chapter Thirty-One

JANUARY 1978

AN ALUMINUM FENCE TWICE AS TALL AS ME SURROUNDED THE camp. Two guards stood by the gate.

I stared in shock. "Is this a prison?"

"The sign reads So Khao Toe." Uncle pointed at the placard on the left side of the gate. "I hope we're not prisoners. I expected to go to Ban Vinai Refugee Camp."

Pheng lived in Ban Vinai. How would we get there?

We got out of the taxi and passed through the gate. The sun moved toward the west. Barracks made of timber and corrugated metal roofs and stalls selling food lined each side of the dirt road. Small tents of blue and gray tarpaulin sheets tied to poles crowded what little space remained.

Groups of refugees with hollow eyes crowded around us. I scanned the crowd. If Toua was alive, we should find him at this camp. I hoped to find someone from the group we had traveled with. A Thai guard shouted at the people to back away. A middle-aged man stepped in and called out for Uncle. The men shook hands with tears in their eyes. The man was Uncle's cousin, Chue Xiong, who had arrived at the camp two weeks earlier. He said the camp was overcrowded. The officers couldn't assign anymore sleeping quarters, so everyone had to share the available space. Chue was willing to share his with our two families. But there was very little space, so Mother didn't accept his offer. We would look for an empty spot somewhere.

"I'll see you and your family around," Kou told me, then left with his family.

Between the barracks and tents, every inch of space seemed occupied. I studied the small place given to the refugees, noticing the empty land beyond the camp's borders. Why didn't the Thai expand this camp?

A woman about Mother's age approached. "Hello, I'm Aunt Tong Chao. We live in the tent near the tree." She pointed to a blue tarpaulin sheet tied to four poles. "For the time being you can share our space."

"Thank you," said Mother gratefully.

The crowd began to disperse. Mother called out, "Has anyone heard or seen a man by the name of Toua Vang?"

Several people shook their heads. Pa and Mother looked at each other. What happened to him? I held back a sob. My family followed Aunt Tong Chao to her tent.

"Wait!"

We turned to the familiar male voice. I burst into tears. Toua ran up to Pa and hugged her.

"I can't believe this!" Toua cried.

It was rare for couples to hug each other in public, but the past four nights had been an eternity and our emotions got the best of us. A group of people gathered around the family like they had never seen a couple embrace before. It was a special moment for us all.

When Toua finally released Pa, he saw Mother with the infant.

"You gave birth!" he shouted.

"Yes." Tears brimmed in Pa's eyes.

Grinning, Toua took his son from Mother. He cuddled and kissed the child. "This is incredible. I'm not dreaming, right?"

"You're not dreaming, son," said Mother in a joyful voice. "Nou went to the village and got us food and clean water. She made a raft, came to Thailand, and got us a canoe."

"Without her, we wouldn't be here," Pa said.

Toua stared at me. "Unbelievable! I am embarrassed. I don't deserve to be a son. I have great respect for you, my sister. I now believe girls can do anything if given the opportunity."

I felt as light as air. "I didn't have a choice," I murmured.

Now that he was alive and well, I wanted to slap him for not returning for us.

"Thank you. You did an exceptional job." Toua shifted his attention to Nhia and stroked his hair. "You made it."

"Uncle," Nhia said with more breath and life than I had seen in him since we began our journey. For the first time, I believed he would be all right.

"Uncle loves you." Toua looked around at us. "Now that we're together again, everything will be all right. We'll find a place. I slept by the fence last night."

"We're going to my tent," said Aunt Tong Chao.

Aunt Tong Chao's son, Khue Lee and his wife, Mor, greeted us when we arrived at the tent. They had two young children. Aunt Tong Chao's husband died in combat.

While we rested with the Lee family, Toua left for the office to register us. I studied my surroundings. People were packed into every corner of the camp. Some men, women, and children sat on rattan mats inside the buildings while others rested in their tents. Some people were at the stalls, along the dirt road, buying food. My stomach growled.

"What food are they selling in the stalls, Aunt Tong Chao?" I asked.

"The Thai vendors sell meat, vegetables, fruit, and sweets. Go check it out," she said.

"I don't have money."

Her brow furrowed. "Oh dear. We just had breakfast at 10:00. We won't get dinner until 5:00."

"How do you know time? Do you have a watch?" I asked.

"There's a clock over there." She pointed at a round dial hanging by a pole near the office. "My son taught me the numbers."

I had heard of clocks for telling time, but I had never seen one. I couldn't wait for Toua to come back from the office. He knew numbers and could read and write some basic words in Laotian.

Toua finally returned with a rattan mat, a blue tarpaulin sheet, poles, two small blankets, and five bowls.

"What are the bowls for?" I asked.

"To get food later. I registered us and filled out a few forms."

"Good."

Khue helped Toua put up our tent. Then, finally, we asked Toua to explain why he abandoned us. He explained that he had fainted on the Thai shore. A family found him and took him to the hospital. An officer had just brought him to the camp last night. He still had a stomachache and diarrhea. He had been in the latrine when we arrived in the camp. My anger faded. He hadn't meant to leave us alone. He had been struggling, too.

Toua and I went to the hanging clock. He taught me how to tell time. I felt fortunate to have the ability to learn quickly. The more I knew, the better for all of us.

At 5:00 the food truck came, and all the people, mostly Hmong and a few Laotians, got in two long lines for food. I didn't see Wa Meng's family or any of the people who came with us during the trek. A lump rose in my throat. What happened to them? I kissed Nhia on the forehead, thankful for having him.

Kou was further ahead in line, but he came over and joined us. He shook hands with Toua. Mother told Toua all that Kou had done for us, and Toua thanked him.

Kou turned to me. "Look at you. This is the first time I see your face bright and eyes dancing in delight. When I met you, your face and eyes were filled with worry."

"My brother is in charge now, and my mother is better," I said.

"Come to Uncle, Nhia." Kou held out his arms for Nhia.

Nhia cried and turned away. He never liked strangers.

At the food truck, I gave the server two bowls. I carried Nhia on my back to free up my hands for the bowls. We no longer had the baby carrier, and it was hard to balance him. With only one arm, Mother couldn't help, and Toua had his hands full with bowls for himself and Pa. Kou laughed and carried Nhia's bowl back to the tent for us.

My bowl of soup was mostly liquid with some rice, a few pieces of chopped chicken, and shredded Napa cabbage. I was so hungry that the soup didn't fill me up. I waited, but with so many people, the chance to refill my bowl didn't come. The United Nations High Commission for Refugees (UNHCR), as the people said, paid for the food. It seemed the UNHCR cared enough to save the refugees but not enough to satisfy their hunger.

Shortly after dinner, I started to have abdominal cramps. I ran to the toilet and found it overflowing. I covered my nose, but the odor made me gag. The contents in my stomach spilled out of my mouth like a waterfall. I suddenly needed to relieve myself and looked around. The camp's pool where they stored the liquid and solid waste was nearby. I ran there.

Many people crowded the place. Each person had their own

small area covered on four sides with cloth to keep them private while they relieved themselves. A woman in her forties allowed me to share her space and relieve myself. The camp's pool of human waste was the stinkiest place I had ever encountered.

As daylight disappeared, Nhia asked again for his mother.

"He will keep asking if we don't tell him the truth." Mother stroked Nhia's hair. "Your mother and grandpa are gone to a place far, far away. You won't see them again, but Aunty Nou and Grandma are here for you. We love you."

"Mom," Nhia cried. "I want my mom."

I wanted my sister, too. Tears pricked my eyes. I had to be strong for Nhia. "If you stop crying, I'll tell you the owl story, and many more."

I held Nhia close until he stopped crying. Then I told him folktales until he fell asleep. Thankfully, Nhia loved stories as much as I did. The stories strengthened the bond between us.

At 10:00 p.m., the camp's electrical lights were turned off, forcing us to sleep. Many slept on the dirt road. Without a country of our own, we were like livestock, locked in a pen with no place to go. So Khao Toe fed us and was a sanctuary, but it was also like a prison.

The next morning at 9:00 a.m., a guard announced on the intercom that So Khao Toe was filled to capacity. In a few days, people would be transferred to Ban Vinai Refugee Camp, the largest camp in Loei province. Most refugees lived there.

I couldn't wait. I was desperate to get out of the stinking camp. Hopefully, we'd find Pheng in Ban Vinai.

Chapter Thirty-Two

A FEW DAYS LATER, SEVERAL BUSES PARKED ON THE ROAD OUTSIDE the wall that surrounded the refugee camp. My family and Kou's were among the first fifty families to leave that morning, and we were on the same bus. More would leave the next day. I experienced no motion sickness this time. I enjoyed the bus ride and wondered about Ban Vinai. Would it be crowded like So Khao Toe? Would we find Pheng there?

Kou sat in front of my family, and he often turned to check on us.

"He likes you," Mother whispered in my ear. "He's a good man. You two should talk. Get to know each other."

"I'm not marrying, remember? I promised to take care of you."

"You must get married. I want grandchildren. He seems like the kind of man that would let me live with you. You can get married and still care for me."

I hadn't thought about that. I'd love to have a man helping. Kou was thoughtful and caring. Maybe he could be a good husband and son-in-law, but I was young and wanted to go to school.

"I don't know, Mother. I'll think about it," I told her.

No one had a watch. We traveled what seemed a long time. I estimated the time to be past noon when the bus finally slowed and turned onto a gravel road in a valley surrounded by sprawling hills of dried grass. The driver announced we had arrived at the camp. Ahead, were fences made of barbed wire instead of aluminum walls.

The road led to a market. Uncle Chong Doua, who had been to the camp once, whispered that it was a Thai market that closed at noon. The consumers were mostly refugees. As the bus moved slowly through the market, I saw a variety of closed stores. Candies, clothes, shoes, and other goods were visible through the rolling gates. The market was bigger than any I had ever seen.

Rows of corrugated aluminum roof buildings with thatch huts stretched as far as I could see. The buses drove past a couple of barracks. A placard was mounted near a wooden fence. It had writing in Laotian and other languages.

Toua read aloud, "Hospital."

Our bus slowed and parked on the side of the road with the other buses. A crowd of people waited on the other side of the road to see the newcomers. I searched for Pheng.

A Hmong officer, wearing a yellow uniform and a helmet, stepped in front of the impatient crowd. Through his bullhorn, he announced, "If you're a relative, a family member, or a friend of someone on the bus, you may take them home with you. Just make sure to bring them to the UNHCR office to register them."

The officer then stepped onto the bus. "Welcome to Ban Vinai. If you have no friends or family members in this camp and don't know where to go, come and see me or the officers so we can assign your family to a center."

Then the officer moved on to the next bus to deliver the

information. Having a Hmong officer speaking to us gave me hope and eased my anxiety.

Out on the road, joyful shouts and cries echoed everywhere. The families on my bus quickly merged with the crowd as their family members stepped up to take them home. Kou's cousin came, but he wouldn't leave until he knew where we would be placed. We stood on the dirt road unclaimed. I had Nhia on my back. Where was Pheng? We gazed in every direction, searching for a familiar face.

"Uncle Cher Moua!" Finally, Toua spotted someone we knew. "Over here!"

Uncle hurried toward us and shook hands with Toua. "I'm happy your family made it," Uncle said.

Toua nodded. His eyes filled with tears.

"*Niam tij*," Uncle called Mother. "Where's brother Wa Shoua?"

"I'll tell you when we get to your house," Mother said softly.

"Are you Der?" Uncle asked me.

"I'm Nou. Der's younger sister."

"Whose child are you carrying?"

"Der's son."

"Where's she?"

"She's not here." My voice quavered. The questions were so hard, and none of us wanted to answer them.

Uncle's brow furrowed. "Let's go to my house."

"Uncle," said Kou. "Can I have your address so I can visit Nou's family later?"

They shook hands, and Uncle gave Kou his address. Kou and his family left. Uncle led us to his home. Uncle Cher Moua was Father's cousin who shared the same clan. In his fifties, he still looked young. His broad, bright face and sparkling eyes made him look healthy and fit.

"How did you know we were coming?" Toua asked.

"There were announcements that a group from So Khao

Toe was coming," said Uncle. "I stopped by to check for any relatives."

"Nou!"

I spun to see who had shouted. Pheng ran toward us. He looked handsome with a short sleeved light blue shirt and black plants, not the traditional clothes he had worn in Laos. Smiling broadly, he greeted Toua first with a handshake. It was the proper way to greet the men first. He looked for Father, then his smile faded.

Pheng glanced at Mother, then to me and Pa. He checked the people over again, then stared at Mother incredulously. "Aunty, where is Der and Uncle Wa Shoua?"

Mother's chin trembled. Pheng bit his lip and shook his head, backing away.

Toua put a hand on Pheng's shoulder and said, "We're sorry."

"Der's married?" Pheng asked.

My brother shook his head. "No."

"She's missing?" Pheng's voice was tight. "I've been waiting for her all these years. Please tell me what happened to her."

Mother touched Pheng's hair. "I'm sorry. She and Uncle Wa Shoua have left us."

Pheng dropped to his knees. Toua quickly pulled him to his feet, and they cried together with Pheng's arms around Toua's shoulders for support. It was too much for me, and my own grief crashed over me again.

"I'm so sorry that Der's gone," I cried. "I have your son."

Pheng turned to me with red eyes. Then his eyes were upon Nhia. "My son?" Pheng extended his arms to the child. "Come to daddy."

Nhia cried and clung to me.

"He's scared of you," I said. "It'll take time."

"Come with us to my home," Uncle said to Pheng. "You need to spend time with the family so the child will know you."

Pheng nodded. Eyes still wet, we walked quickly and quietly on a dirt road just wide enough for a bus to pass through. Rows of barracks built with cement walls and corrugated aluminum roofs and thatched huts lined each side of the road.

Uncle lived on Center 2, Section 3, and he led us to Barrack 4. At Room 2, Uncle's wife Hlee, daughter Yer, and two sons, Neng and Kai, greeted us. Yer was shorter and two years younger than me. We looked similar with brown eyes, olive skin, and waist-length black hair.

The families in the next rooms came to greet us, as well. Emotions churned in me. I felt relief and joy to be safe and to see relatives, but the grief of loss felt greater than ever. For the first time in many weeks, I felt safe to express my feelings. Mother took Nhia, and I wailed and wailed until my voice was hoarse. My cousin, Yer, coaxed me out of the room for fresh air.

As I caught my breath, Yer gave me a tour around the section. Each barrack was divided into ten small, four-walled rooms. Some rooms had large families of parents, grandparents, and children living together. Most of the children were out on the sidewalks. Some played tops and tag while others socialized with their friends. Younger children clung to their mothers who sat on footstools stitching cloths.

"What are they stitching?" I asked.

"They're making *paj ntaub*," said Yer. "There are no jobs, so women are embroidering story cloths of Hmong lives in the fields and their history of fleeing to Thailand. They also make Hmong textiles of many patterns. They sell the *paj ntaub* to foreigners who come to the camp."

Men sat on foot stools and chatted. It had been a long time since I had seen men socializing with one another. Every person I met welcomed me to the new place. These people spoke without fear. They seemed happy enough. They had a place to sleep and food to eat.

That evening, Yer and I cooked rice and stir-fried bok choy with some dashes of salt. It brought many memories of my cooking with Der back in Laos.

After supper Pheng begged Mother to tell him what happened to Der. Everyone sat on the cement floor in the room and listened attentively.

"She was shot," said Mother. "This is what she said to me. *'Tell Pheng that I love him. I wore the blouse he sent because I thought I'd see him tomorrow. I wanted to look beautiful for him. Now it'll go with me to the afterlife. He'll always be in my heart. I love him very much.'*"

"I love her, too." Pheng buried his face in his hands, shaken by deep, racking sobs. "I want to die!"

"No." Mother smoothed his hair. "We'll find you a beautiful girl. Don't ever mention death."

I wanted to comfort him, too—to stroke his hair and tell him he had a bright future ahead with his son, but I held back. If I showed too much sympathy, Pheng might get the impression that I was interested in him.

"You can't die," I said. "Your son needs you."

He turned to Nhia and me with red and puffy eyes. His gaze locked on us, and he gave us a half smile. Throughout the evening, Pheng reached out to Nhia. Each time, Nhia cried and turned away. Pheng left before bedtime.

Chapter Thirty-Three

The morning air chilled Nhia and me. We joined Toua and Uncle by the small charcoal stove in the lean-to cooking area for warmth. Made of a grass roof and bamboo walls, the lean-to was attached to Uncle Moua's room. Pheng walked in and shook hands with Toua and Uncle.

"No school?" Uncle asked.

"I'm taking the day off. I'd like to take Toua's family to register today," said Pheng. "Sorry, I'm early. I just don't like to wait in line."

"It's perfect," Toua said. "Thank you."

"You're welcome."

Pheng stretched his arms to Nhia who sat beside me. Nhia's eyes widened, and he ran out the door. I chased him. Pheng followed us. He reached for Nhia, and Nhia shrank away, crying. I picked him up and held him tightly.

"Don't be scared," I said. "He's your father."

Pheng took a small bag of candies from his packet. He opened the bag, picked an orange bean-size candy, and held it out to Nhia. Nhia eyed the candy for a long time. Finally, he looked up at Pheng, who was an arm length away, then pressed his face against my shoulder. I took the candy from Pheng and put it in Nhia's mouth. Nhia chewed on it and smiled. He pointed at the bag in Pheng's hand but wouldn't look at Pheng.

"I want to hold and kiss him." Pheng's voice was deep and pleasant.

"Be patient," I said.

"Nou, thank you for taking such good care of him. You saved his life. I am forever in your debt."

I locked eyes with him. "If Der hadn't said to bring him to you, I wouldn't let you near him. I'd like to slap you hard for the pain you caused her."

Pheng flinched. "I'm sorry. I understand the shame and embarrassment Der lived through." He looked at the ground. "I have suffered as much as Der, in a different way."

"You've proved you love her, and that eases some of my anger. I've been taking care of your son since the day he was born. But I do it for my sister, not for you."

"I'm sorry for the pain you went through," he replied. "You can hit me all you want if it will make you feel better."

Toua stepped outside. "We are ready to go."

Pheng led us to the United Nations High Commission for Refugees (UNHCR) barrack north of the dusty soccer field. As we crossed the field, he explained that each center had a team of players, and they practiced in the field almost every evening. There were four teams for the four centers, and they had their first soccer competitions during the New Year celebration, which was in late December. The UNHCR building had antique white stucco siding with a red tile metal roof. A crowd of people waited outside the door.

"There's no room inside," said Pheng.

Toua and Pheng stepped up to the Thai worker at the window to sign us in.

When they returned, Toua said, "Now we wait to have our picture taken for our BV."

"What's BV?" I asked.

"Identity card. BV stands for Ban Vinai," said Pheng. "When you have your BV, you are officially a refugee, and you'll be provided with food and housing."

When our turn came, we entered a foyer with an old wooden desk stacked with paperwork. A Thai man sat behind the desk. He was a Joint Voluntary Agency (JVA) worker. We sat on a bench against the wall.

The registrar gave us each a card with a number on it and pinned the card to our shirts. Toua's was number 1.1, Pa's number 1.2, TouZou's, being their son, number 1.3, Mother's number 1.4, and mine was number 1.5. Nhia was excluded because Pheng wanted to add him to his family.

The man gave Toua a sign that read, "BV003560." Toua held the sign in front of him. The man took a picture of the whole family. A minute later, we saw ourselves in the black and white picture. I gaped. It was like magic. How did a camera work? Whoever created it must be a genius.

The registrar took another picture of us, then we followed him to a room where he gave the pictures to a JVA worker. The worker talked to both Mother and Toua and filled out a couple forms. He then stapled the two pictures to the two stack of paperwork and gave one stack to Toua. He kept the other stack in the office. We were officially refugees.

That evening, Yer and I went to the Section 3 water station on the other side of the road. The people ahead of us filled their containers from a faucet connected by pipes connected to tanks placed on a tall wooden platform.

"Yer," I said, as we waited in line, "I heard the refugees can go to America. Do you know the process?"

"No. My father doesn't want to go to America and doesn't talk about it."

"Why doesn't your father want to go?"

"He wants to return to Laos. General Vang Pao told him

that there would be peace soon. When there is peace in Laos, all the refugees here will return."

"Return?" I scoffed. "Never will I return to that country. My father told me that America is a rich country. Than Pop said education is free and every child goes to school. Who would not want to go there?"

Yer turned to me. "Who's Than Pop?"

"You don't know him?" I asked, surprised. "He's an American."

"America may not be what you think. I heard it's bad there."

I drew in a sharp breath. "Tell me more."

"I don't know a whole lot. My uncle Thong Ma lives in America and sends us money all the time, but my father never says anything good about it."

"If Uncle Thong Ma sends you money from America, he must be doing well. What's bad about it?"

"Sorry, I don't know. You'd be better off asking someone else, but not my father. He'd convince you not to go. I've seen that happen." Yer paused. "A few things you should know about the camp. You need to be careful about the ten o'clock evening curfew. If you are caught after that, the officers beat you up and put you in jail, and I know a few women who were raped. We don't have many rights or protections here."

I nodded, rubbing my hands as anxiety kicked in. I thought we were safe here.

We filled our containers and carried them home on our backs. When we arrived, Uncle and Toua were gone. Pheng sat on a wooden stool outside the lean-to. Mother chased Nhia and caught him. He laughed out loud, and Pheng smiled as he watched his son play.

I set the container down next to the earthen water jar and caught my breath. "Pheng."

He turned to me, his eyes bright and warm. "You're back."

"I want to go to America, but Yer said it is a bad country. What do you know about it?"

"My uncle lives in America and has told me a lot. Also, I learned about it in my English class."

"What's an 'English class?'" I asked.

"A class where you learn to read and write in English. It's a paid course. I quit because it got expensive."

I gawked. "School isn't free in this camp?"

"The regular classes like math, science, Hmong, Thai, and Lao languages are free."

I nodded in relief. "Good."

"School is only a half day," Pheng continued. "There aren't enough classrooms, so you choose either morning or afternoon classes. English classes are taught at the instructors' homes at various times."

I took a stool from nearby and pulled it close to him. Avoiding eye contact as always, my eyes were on the earthen water jar. "Tell me about America."

"I heard rumors that there are crimes, prostitution, and discrimination of race in America. But no country is perfect. My uncle has a good job, and his children have a good education."

"We should all go to America."

He nodded. "Yes. The Americans are currently taking applications. It's our chance."

Excitement bubbled over in me. "How do we apply?"

Pheng chuckled. "You sound like you used to."

"I know." I looked down. "I was loud. I guess my old habits are returning."

"Never mind," he said. "To answer your question, we'll go to the UNHCR office to fill out a form."

I looked up. "Should we go tomorrow?"

"The Americans will be here for a while, so there's time. You just got here. We can wait a couple days."

"I want to go to school. Where do I register?" I was afraid to ask too many questions, but he didn't seem irritated.

"I can help you, but one thing at a time. First, let's get your family settled with a home and food. Don't overwhelm yourself."

"All right," I said, though I couldn't wait to register my family to go to America.

We had to get out of the camp before we were forced to go back to Laos. Pheng's uncle's children were getting a good education. I wanted one, too.

Chapter Thirty-Four

UNCLE FOUND A ROOM FOR MY FAMILY IN SECTION 3, BARRACK 15, Room 1. It had four cement walls and a hard cement floor, a lean-to, and a toilet attached to the back. Our room was one section away from Uncle's.

As the leader of our barrack, Xao Chia Moua supervised food distribution and hauled the food, except rice, home in his two-wheeled wagon. We picked up our rations from him.

Meat, chicken, or fish was on Monday. Vegetables, Napa cabbage, or Chinese broccolis, were on Thursday. Rice came only once a month, and every family collected their ration directly from the distribution station. For this month, people shared their rice with my family. Next month, we'd get our own ration.

In addition to our new room, we received donations of clothes from the UNHCR and silverware, pots, pans, and plastic containers from Uncle. He was fortunate his brother in America sent him money to spend. My family received no financial help.

Pheng came at mid-afternoon and, as usual, brought eggs for Nhia and Wai noodles for the family for supper. I was embroidering, so Mother took the food inside the lean-to, leaving Nhia outside the door. Pheng gave Nhia a candy. Nhia took it and ran to me.

"He still doesn't like me," Pheng complained.

"Candies aren't enough," I said. "You need to spend time with him."

"How? This is the fifth day, and he still won't look at me." Pheng's expression clouded. "I have to add Nhia to our family before applying to America. My parents want me to register soon since the deadline is in two weeks. We must go this round or wait seven to eight months for the next round."

My pulse quickened. "My family has to leave, too. Seven to eight more months is too long."

"Can you bring Nhia to the UNHCR office tomorrow?" Pheng asked. "We'll take a picture with him."

I nodded.

"Come around nine a.m.," he said.

"You're skipping school?"

"I can go to school in America. Here is just temporary."

"Yer told me I don't need school now, but I want to read my father's paper. Can I take a Hmong literacy class?" I asked.

He nodded. "Yes. You need to learn Hmong. I'll help you register tomorrow after we are done."

After supper, Pheng tried to play peekaboo with Nhia. Nhia cried, and Pheng left with tears in his eyes.

THE SUN SAT HIGH IN THE SKY WHEN NHIA AND I ARRIVED AT THE UNHCR building the next morning to find Pheng's family waiting for us. He had five younger siblings, two brothers, and three sisters. The family greeted me and seemed nice and friendly. I had seen his sister, Maihoua, a couple of times back in the village. Seeing Maihoua brought memories of Der. They had been friends. I blinked back tears.

"Nou, you have grown," Maihoua said. "You are as beautiful as your sister."

I smiled shyly. "You have grown, too."

"Thank you for bringing Nhia here." Pheng's mother, Aunt Chong Tou, extended her hands to Nhia. He drew back and wailed. She stepped away.

"Sorry," I said. "He had bad experiences on the trek, the shootings, and starvation. The Laotian and Thai men scared him."

Tears appeared in Aunt Chong Tou's eyes. "I can't imagine the horrible things he saw and lived through. Poor child."

"How are we going to get this child into our picture?" asked Pheng's father.

Nhia wouldn't stop crying and buried his face in my shoulder.

"We'll have to have Nou hold him and be in the picture with us," Pheng said.

"I can't be in the picture," I said quickly. "I'm not part of your family."

Uncle Chong Tou shook his head. "It's not going to work today. We'll go home and think this over."

The family left. Pheng led Nhia and me to the shed next to the post office by the soccer field. It wasn't far. The school was a dark brown woodshed with a corrugated metal roof.

"This is the Hmong class," Pheng said. "You two stay put while I talk to the teacher."

Pheng emerged from the building. "This class is full. The teacher said the session at eight o'clock tomorrow morning has seats open. You can show up tomorrow with a notebook and pen."

I could go to school? I couldn't believe it.

"Is it the same teacher?" I asked.

"No. Each session has a different volunteer."

On the way home, we stopped at Center 2 Market. The

aroma of grilled meat and noodle soups filled the air, making my mouth water. Shoppers crowded the market. At a Thai stall, two people stood in line waiting for papaya salads. Other stalls sold gai choy, lemon grass, bok choy, bitter lemon, ginger, green onion, cilantro, watermelon, yellow mangos, and bananas.

Pheng took us to a booth. "I haven't eaten anything today," he said. "Let's eat before we go."

"Nhia and I ate before we came. We'll wait on the road for you."

"You are eating with me. I want Nhia and you to try *fawm*, a rice noodle. It's very good."

As the oldest son, he had money from his parents. I didn't want him spending that money on me. "I'm not hungry," I lied.

"Hungry or not, you are going in with me. Come on."

I couldn't resist the savory smell. I followed Pheng into the booth. A family occupied one of the two tables, and we took the empty one. Pheng gazed at me as we waited. I played with Nhia to avoid making eye contact. I wasn't shy talking to Pheng, but I felt nervous around him. It was different than in the village when he was so annoying to me. Times had changed. I started to like kind, caring, and handsome men. I thought of Kou. How was he doing? Why hadn't he visited?

"You have grown as beautiful as your sister," Pheng said softly.

I wasn't beautiful like my sister, but I wasn't ugly either. I liked myself for myself.

"We are different, but you are still the same handsome man," I said. "You'll find a girl easily."

"There are plenty of girls but finding the right one is hard."

The *fawm* in beef broth with chili, fish sauce, green onion, and cilantro was delicious. Nhia and I ate everything and drank all the liquid in our bowls. Two bowls cost Pheng six bahts. He paid with a twenty baht bill and received his change.

On the road, he grasped my hand. His big, warm hand on mine generated sparks within me, so I pulled away. He grasped my hand again and put a ten baht bill on my palm.

"Take it and buy drinks for you and my son."

I shook my head. "I can't take money from anyone."

The corners of his mouth pulled downward. "You can take from me. It's for my son."

He stood so close his warm breath bathed my face. I hated the butterfly feeling in my stomach. It was the same feeling I had for Kou. I took the money and stepped away from him. Why was this happening? I must not allow kindness or a handsome face to interfere with my dreams and my promise to my mother.

At home, Pheng told Toua and Mother that Nhia had not been added to his family. He sat with his hands clenched in front of him. "If only his mother were here."

Mother sat beside him and smoothed his hair. "We're sorry."

"Be patient. Things will get better," Toua said, "You can sleep with us tonight. You should sleep with us every night, so Nhia knows he's safe with you. Please make this your home."

"Thank you," Pheng said.

He watched Nhia and me, teary-eyed. I wasn't sure if he wished I was Der or felt bad he didn't know how to relate to his child.

Chapter Thirty-Five

Pheng didn't have to buy us food the next evening. We received five tunas from our ration. Not bound to any responsibilities, Pheng cleaned the fish for me to deep fry, and fetched water from the station. Memories of Der's happiness sent thick waves of grief over me. I missed her so much. I hated the war for shattering her dream. My chest heaved and tears filled my eyes.

Pheng frowned. "Are you all right?"

"I miss my sister," I whispered.

"You know how I feel."

He put a hand on my shoulder, and I brushed it off, not to be rude but to avoid sparks. I did appreciate Pheng's help because my mother couldn't do much with one hand. She was adjusting and worked hard on using her one hand. Toua was always busy caring for TouZou while Pa stitched *paj ntaub*, so she could earn money for food and clothes.

I was frying fish in the lean-to when, outside, Mother said Kou's name. I hurried to the door. Kou was shaking hands with Toua and Pheng. Most people stayed outside under the shade because it was cooler. The men talked for a while, then Kou came inside, smiling.

"Hello." I returned the smile. "How have you been?"

"Great," Kou said. "I wanted to come sooner but have been busy with school, adjusting to the new place, and exploring the camp. Your uncle told me your new address."

"You are already enrolled in school?" I asked.

"Yes, since the first day. There's nothing else to do, and I like to keep myself busy."

"Nice. I'm so glad to see you again." I flipped the fish in the pan. "Sit." I pointed at the wooden stool by the door.

Mother and Nhia came inside.

"Hi Nhia," said Kou.

Nhia turned away, grabbed Mother's leg, and held tight.

"He's still afraid of strangers," I said.

Mother chatted with Kou while I cooked. When the fish were done, I set the small round bamboo table in the dining area. On the table, I put a bowl of rice, a bowl of fried fish, a bowl of water, and three spoons for the three men. According to tradition, they ate first. We would eat whatever food remained.

I watched with Nhia on my lap. Kou ate a little and hardly talked. He seemed uncomfortable. I wondered if Pheng intimidated him. Pheng acted like he was part of the family, which he wasn't.

After dinner, Kou winked at me, and I had a feeling he wanted to talk. I told Mother I was going to take a bath at the well. I took a set of clothes and a bucket and winked at Kou and left. I strolled in the direction of the well. Kou caught up with me, and we continued toward a nearby garden.

"Thanks for taking this time with me," Kou said. "My family lives in Center 4. It's a long walk here. Do you mind if I ask you a question about Pheng?"

"No. Why?"

"I understand that he's Nhia's father and he's here for the child. What I don't understand is he seems really interested in you. His eyes were on you almost all the time. I'm not kidding."

Interesting. Kou didn't miss anything.

"He loved my sister very much. He's broken-hearted. He might show interest in me because I'm Der's sister and Nhia's aunt. Nothing else." I stopped walking. "You and I are not boyfriend and girlfriend. I hope you aren't jealous."

"We aren't officially boyfriend and girlfriend, but I liked you the minute I saw you at the shore," he said.

I started walking again. "With the messy hair, dirty face, and blood-stained clothes?"

"Yes." He chuckled. "You were dirty but still beautiful. I loved how you protected Nhia. At first, I thought he was your child. When I heard him mumble Aunty, I knew he wasn't yours."

"Do you notice everything?" I asked.

He stepped in front of me. His lips curved upward in a small smile. "Yes. I immediately loved everything about you. I didn't say so because I want to show you through actions."

"Why tell me this now?" I smiled.

"Because I don't want to lose you to Pheng." He cleared his throat. "Nou, I love you. I'll come every evening from now on."

Having Pheng around was already irritating. Adding Kou to my evening would make things worse. I didn't want to be rude, but I needed to be clear. "I don't mind you coming every day, but I have things to do and may not be able to talk to you. How about three or four times a week?"

A moment of silence passed.

"If Pheng can come every day, why can't I?" he asked. "I can help you with chores. Don't you need help?"

I wanted to tell him that Pheng had a reason, but he had a reason, too. My family owed his family money. His family was a big factor in saving our lives, so I must choose my words carefully not to upset him.

"I won't say no to help. I also don't want to be a burden. Can we talk about this another time? I'm going to take a bath."

"All right," he said. "I'm going home then. See you tomorrow."

I nodded. "Good-bye."

"Good-bye."

Pheng stood outside the door with a dark expression when I returned home.

"Nhia was looking for you." His voice was filled with sadness.

"That kid is always looking for me. I need a break from him."

"I'm sorry. He's a burden."

"He's not a burden," I said.

I walked past him and put the half-full bucket of water by the door. Nhia ran to me, and I picked him up and kissed him. "I'm going to give you a bath," I told him.

Pheng watched me giving Nhia a bath, and he joined us in our story time. I told Nhia stories until he fell asleep on my arms. I laid him on the rattan mat, our sleeping area, and covered him with a cloth.

"Do you do this for Nhia every night?" Pheng asked.

"Yes. Every night."

His eyes widened.

Mother and I each lay beside Nhia for the night. Pheng slept in the other corner of the room, on the floor like everyone else. Our family couldn't afford bamboo cots.

I woke to Nhia's wail. It was the middle of the night, and I didn't want to get up, but I had to quiet him before he woke up TouZou.

"I'm here," I soothed.

Nhia crawled to my lap. I rubbed his back. "Go back to sleep."

After Nhia quieted, Pheng whispered across the room, "Does he cry every night?"

"Most nights," Mother said.

The room fell silent, and I went back to sleep.

Chapter Thirty-Six

When the rice was done that following morning, I set the pot on the ground to cool. Pheng entered the lean-to.

"Are you ready?" He checked his watch. "You have twenty minutes to get to your

class."

"I'm ready."

I entered the room to check on Mother and Nhia. They still slept. I grabbed my notebook and pen. Outside the door, Pheng waited.

"I'm going home, so I'll walk with you to your Hmong class," he said. "It's your first day. You need company."

I could probably find my way there, but it wouldn't hurt to have him show me again.

I nodded. "All right."

As we walked, Pheng said, "Nou, I couldn't sleep last night after Nhia woke us up. I thought hard about Nhia's and my future. I can't raise him without you."

"You can. It'll be difficult, but not impossible. My mother and I will help as much as we can."

"You can help now, but what about the future? America is

huge. If we don't live near each other, how are you going to help?"

I stopped and turned to him. "You are right. We have to live near each other. Well, either you and Nhia move near us, or we move near you."

"I have a plan." Pheng's eyes sparkled.

"What is it?"

"I'm sorry to say this right now, but this is the only time I have with you one-on-one." Pheng took a heavy breath. "If you marry me and be Nhia's mother, we all will be together."

I couldn't believe my ears. I wouldn't marry my sister's lover. It didn't feel right. Also, marriage wouldn't work as I was bound to my vow to Mother. I turned away and quickened my pace. Pheng sped after me.

"You love him and want the best for him," he said. "So do I. Together, we'll be the best parents for him. He needs us."

Nhia did need two loving and caring parents. Pheng was right about that. Der had asked me to help raise Nhia, and Pheng was caring and handsome, but I wouldn't leave my mother.

"Nhia's lucky to have you as a father. Your caring means a lot to me," I said. "I'm sorry I can't marry you. I have my mother to care for."

"Your mother will live with us, and I'll help you care for her."

The sincerity in his voice gave me pause. Mother did say that she wanted me to marry and have children.

"That's very nice of you," I said.

He kept pace alongside me. "I mean it. Nhia and your mother need both of us."

I gave him a tight-lipped smile. He smiled back.

"If I decide to get married in the future," I said, "I want my marriage to be out of love, not because I can be a good mother."

He stepped in front of me, and I halted. "I love you. I need you in my life," he said. He grasped my hand. His palm was warm and sweaty. "Nhia is the only memory I have of Der. He's my treasure. I'm sure he's your only memory of Der, too. Together, we'll be a happy family." He squeezed my hand. "Only you can bring Nhia and me happiness."

I pulled free of his hand and began walking again.

"Nou, is Kou your boyfriend?" he asked.

I frowned. "No, why?"

"Kou seems interested in you and jealous when I'm around you."

My head began to throb. I didn't want to talk about Kou. The last thing I wanted was tension between the men. I ran ahead. When I reached the school, I turned and Pheng was gone. Tears filled my eyes. He was serious and seemed desperate for me, but I didn't feel the same way for him. I wished for Der. If she were here, we all would be happy. I'd have more freedom and choices.

A young man glanced at me as he entered the building. I hurried inside. The classroom was once a storage room for the post office. Twenty-four students between the ages of twelve and twenty-five sat on six old wooden benches arranged in rows. Cha Bee Xiong, who was in his late thirties, was our teacher. We called him Teacher Cha Bee.

I had a lot of catching up to do, so I tried to focus. Teacher Cha Bee wrote all the tones, consonants, and vowels on the board for me to copy. After he taught the lesson of the day, he taught me the basics. The same young man from earlier, two seats on my right, glanced at me often.

Toward the end of class, he came over. "Hello. My name is Xue Lor. What's your name?"

"Nou Vang," I said.

"I can help you if you need help studying at home."

Heaven, I didn't need three men at my house. "Very kind of you, but I don't need help."

The teacher dismissed us. I hurried out the door. Xue caught up with me.

"Are you new to the camp?" he asked.

"Yes."

"You are beautiful. Do you have a boyfriend?"

"Yes," I said.

"He's lucky. If I wasn't leaving for America soon, I'd steal you from him," he laughed.

"When are you going?" I asked.

"Our interview is next week. My father was a soldier, which makes us a top priority. Is your family going?"

"Yes, but we haven't applied yet."

"You better do it soon before they close registration."

"I will. Thanks for telling me."

At home, I put my notebook away. Pa sat in the shade of the lean-to embroidering and Toua and TouZou sat nearby. Thank goodness Toua was home. Usually, he and TouZou were gone with Uncle during the day. Nhia and Mother were by the door. Everyone was here. A great time for a family talk.

"Toua, Mother, and *tis nyab*, can we have a talk inside?" I asked.

"Sure," Pa said. "Do you have important news?"

"Yes."

The family gathered in the lean-to.

"We have to go to America," I said. "Toua's home, so today is a good day for us to apply and start the process."

"I'd like to go to America," said Pa. "But who would sponsor us? We have no relatives there."

"Pheng said churches and organizations usually sponsor refugees. A church sponsored his uncle. I'm sure they will sponsor our family."

"We're not going," Toua said firmly.

I stared at him open-mouthed, and it took me a moment to get the word out. "Why?"

"General Vang Pao is going to return and there will soon be peace in Laos. We'll go back."

I shook my head. "No. We are not going back."

"I'm not going to America," said Toua. "It's terrible there. White people hate other races, and they are the majority."

"You believe everything Uncle said," I snapped. "Without a country, we aren't welcome anywhere. We should be glad the United States of America is accepting us. We will have a better life there."

"Nou's right," Pa said. "I want to go to America."

"You're my wife and you stay with me," Toua scolded. "I know what's best for us and our son."

Pa's expression dulled.

"Toua, we've suffered enough. We are going forward," Mother spoke with authority. "Please take us to America."

Silence settled over the family.

Finally, Toua said, "Mother, Uncle and I met with the leaders. There will be peace soon, and we are going back."

"You believe them!" Anger bubbled in my gut. I wouldn't let him keep me from my dream. "There will be no peace, and if the authorities decide to close the camp, we'll be forced to go back. America is our hope, and now is our opportunity."

Toua's brows drew together. "I am a man. I make decisions for the family."

I lifted my chin. "I might be a girl, but I know what's best for us."

He nodded slowly. "You brought the family to Thailand, but that doesn't make you the head of the household. You are not in charge of this family."

I swallowed hard. Slowly, I sucked in a breath to calm myself. "If you don't want to go, Mother and I will go by ourselves."

"No," said Mother quickly. "If we don't have a man, we'd

become objects of scorn. Also, I'm getting old. Without a man, who will provide me a funeral when I die?"

She was right. Everything would be more difficult without Toua. But I wasn't willing to let him determine my fate. "Don't worry, Mother. I will see to your funeral."

"I know you can do anything, but it's not something a woman would do."

"Then, I'll be the first woman to do it because I'm not going to stay in this crowded, stinky place with guards who beat up refugees for no reasons and rape women," I declared.

"It's all right with me if you and Mother want to go now," Toua said. "Pa and I will come later if the situation in Laos doesn't improve."

"If Father were here, he'd want you to leave this place," I said.

Toua scowled. "How do you know?"

"Because he told me that America would give us a better life."

"Son," Mother cried. "You are your father's only son. He wants the best for you."

"I'm choosing what's best for my family," he insisted.

I knew Toua wouldn't listen. As a stepmother, Mother could only give suggestions and advice. She couldn't make him do anything. If I were a son, my mother and I could do anything and go anywhere without her worrying about us becoming objects of scorn. If I were a son, she wouldn't have to worry about her funeral. But I was not a son. I was a daughter. I would do things my way.

Chapter Thirty-Seven

As usual Pheng arrived at midafternoon. He immediately noticed the quiet and tension.

"Is everything all right, Toua?" he asked.

"I'm fine. It's Nou who's unhappy."

I was still angry. I snatched up the bucket of dirty clothes and left for the well. Pheng tagged along.

"What's going on?" he asked.

"Toua's been brainwashed and won't go to America."

"Poor man. He should go. There's nothing here and nothing in Laos for us." He paused. "Nou, marry me, and I'll take you to America."

I glanced at the women stitching in the shade against a nearby lean-to. They didn't seem to notice us.

"I don't have to marry you to go to America," I said in a low voice. "My mother and I will go by ourselves."

"Without a man?" he asked, incredulous.

It would be great to have a man to protect us and assure our safety but not through marriage. I would not get married young. Raising Nhia was difficult enough. I wasn't ready to have children, and I needed time for myself.

"We'll be fine," I said. "I don't think it will be as bad as the trek from Laos."

"Each journey is different. You are an attractive girl. I worry about bad men doing bad things to you, like raping and kidnapping."

"I'll be careful."

We walked in silence.

"Is your mother in agreement?" he asked in a soft voice.

"She'll go wherever I want to go. I decide what's best for us."

"A daughter decides for her mother?" Pheng shook his head.

"What's wrong with that?" I demanded. "Children are to take care of the elderly when they can't help themselves."

"You are right. It's just unusual that a sixteen-year-old girl is making decisions for her mother when her mother is capable of thinking."

"My mother trusts me. I'm her protector, and I took care of her all the way here."

We neared the well. A woman was washing clothes there.

"Pheng, can you go back to the home? I don't want people to think that you are my boyfriend," I said.

He hesitated, then nodded. "All right. I should spend time with Nhia."

After he left, I pulled water from the well with my metal bucket and rope. I cleaned myself. The cool water calmed my anger. I was alone now. I pulled more water and started washing the clothes piece by piece in the shallow basin. A shadow appeared over the basin. I looked up to see Kou standing tall on my right. Like always, he smiled.

I smiled back. "How did you know I was here?" I asked.

"Your mother told me." He glanced around. "It's a perfect time. Just you and me." He squatted next to me. "Each time I see you, you get prettier."

I nudged his elbow. "Liar."

"With food, you are slightly fuller, and your face is brighter."

"You are still the same perfect man each time I see you."

"Can we stay here until evening?" he asked.

"I'd love to, but I have a child and chores. Is your family planning to go to America?"

"Not now, but maybe later. Is your family?" he asked.

"My brother doesn't want to go, but my mother and I want to go."

"If your brother is not ready, you should wait."

I missed the first opportunity that Than Pop offered me. If I missed this second opportunity, would I have luck a third time?

"We aren't safe in this camp, and I'm scared to go back to the country that killed my family." I kept my attention on the clothes. "America is the best option, and we must go now."

"You are right. I didn't think of it before."

I finished my laundry and stood, the wet clothes in my basin.

Kou rose with me and said, "Nou."

I looked up at him. "Yes."

"I'm a little picky and when I find the right person, it's hard to lose her. Would you marry me?"

Shock slipped down my spine. For Pheng and Kou, I was worthy of marrying. My spirits lifted. Kou was the man I wanted to marry, but I bit my bottom lip. I couldn't accept his proposal now. Maybe in the future. I must focus on my dreams, my mother, and Nhia. Kou and his family had done so much for my family. What could I say that wouldn't hurt his feelings?

I sighed. "We have known one another for less than a month. We don't know each other well enough to get married."

"In my heart, I know you are the one. I can't lose you."

I stared at the well, unable to reply.

"I know it's a hard decision," he said softly. "You have Pheng and Nhia."

"It's not Pheng. If I didn't have commitments, I'd marry you. You are a great man with a kind, big heart."

"What commitments?" he asked.

"I must take care of my mother, and I want to go to school to learn to read and write so I can write stories someday. It's my dream."

His mouth twitched with amusement, and he grasped my hands. "Great! You are a smart girl. The girl I'm looking for because I want my wife to have an education. Please marry me. I want to help make your dreams come true. I'll support you one hundred percent and will help take care of your mother. She'll live with us. I promise."

My heart pounded, and heat radiating through my chest. I couldn't think straight. What could be so special about me that both Pheng and Kou would be willing to care for my mother, too? They treated me like I had worth and value. Kou's words touched my heart. I became aware of his warm fingers gently holding mine, and I considered marrying him.

Mother liked him. She would approve. But marriage frightened me. A daughter-in-law had a lot of responsibilities. I already had enough responsibilities on my plate. Our lives weren't stable. If the camp closed down, we could be sent back to Laos. My sister suffered for love and lived in shame. I would not go through the hardship she went through. I would not get married now. I must wait until I had a stable life.

"You are a caring and invaluable friend. I am so lucky to have met you," I said.

His eyes gleamed.

"My mother and I need a man, and your support would be tremendous, but I'm sorry I'm not ready to get married."

A moment of silence passed. Then he asked in a soft voice, "How long do I have to wait?"

"Until I'm ready."

"Promise me you will marry me."

The future was unknown, and I couldn't make more

promises. "I can't promise you because I don't know what will happen. I hope you understand."

A tinge of sadness crossed his face. The half-full water bucket sat near me, and I flicked some water at Kou. He smiled. He dipped a hand into the bucket and splashed me back. I laughed and scooped more water and tossed it at him. Beads of water covered his face. I scooped more water out and splashed him. I quickly emptied the bucket.

"That's not fair," he complained with a laugh.

I smiled and wiped the water off his face with my hands. He looked around, then drew me close. His warm breath bathed my face, and his heart beat in rhythm with mine. Heat flooded through me. I wanted to be in his arms forever. Der had told me that someday I would know love. That moment had arrived and if I wasn't careful, I'd be like her, young and pregnant.

I twisted out of his arms. Luckily no one was around. I couldn't shame my family or myself and must not allow any man to touch me ever again.

Not until I was married.

Chapter Thirty-Eight

Nhia's cry echoed from the alley as Kou and I approached my home. We found Mother outside walking and rocking Nhia on her back. I ran to them and took Nhia. He clung to me, and I stroked his hair.

"What happened?" I asked.

"Pheng tried to hold him and scared him," said Mother.

"I don't understand why Nhia doesn't like him at all," I said. "Where's Pheng?"

"He went to the market for candy."

Kou fished in his pants pocket, pulled out a toy car, and gave it to me. "I bought it for Nhia. I think he might like to play with it."

"Thank you." I showed it to Nhia. "It's a car. You can make it move around."

Nhia stopped crying, and I carried him inside. On the smooth concrete floor, I gave the toy a push and it rolled across the room. Nhia shouted and ran after it.

He gave it a push, and Kou crawled alongside the toy as it moved toward the opposite wall. Nhia followed him. They crawled alongside each other, and Kou cheered and praised

Nhia as they chased the toy. They continued shoving and chasing the toy car together. Their laughter filled the room and echoed outside. Pa peeked at us and smiled.

When Nhia tired, Kou spun the car for him and Nhia watched and screamed in delight. Kou taught him how to do it himself. They played like father and son. Tears pricked the corners of my eyes.

"Kou's good with children," I whispered to Mother, who sat beside me. "Pheng has a lot to learn."

"True. Nhia is more comfortable with Kou because Kou has been with us longer. I'm optimistic that Pheng will soon earn his son's trust."

Pheng arrived with candy in hand. He stared at Kou and Nhia, his face hard.

"You are back at the right time," Mother said. "You should play with Kou and Nhia."

Nhia ran to me and sat on my lap.

"Go show your toy to your father," I said. Nhia pressed his face against my chest. "Pheng, I'd like you to play with him."

"I'd love to, but he doesn't want to play with me." Pheng spoke softly as if he were sick and handed me the candies. "Give them to Nhia. I'm going home. See you tomorrow."

Earlier, he had asked to spend the night with us again, and I was going to tell him to stay. But he looked so tense, I was glad he left because I would have hated to ask the men to leave should tension arise.

Pheng left and Mother followed him.

"I'm sorry," Kou said. "Pheng doesn't like me."

"He's unhappy that he can't get his son to like him," I said.

Kou stayed for dinner, chatting with Toua and playing with Nhia. He left before the curfew at ten p.m.

Nhia wasn't ready to sleep and still played with the toy in the lean-to. Mother and I watched him. The flame in the oil lamp swayed slightly as the wind swooshed through.

"Pheng likes you," Mother said. "He's jealous of Kou."

"He told you that?" I asked.

"Yes. Kou and Pheng are decent men, and I approve of them both. Who do you like best?"

Why did she want to know? I was hesitant but had to tell her the truth. "Pheng's more handsome, but Kou sees me as I am and understands me. We have more in common. I like him more." I paused. "If I have to get married, I want a man who loves us both and will help me care for you. Who do you think suits us best?"

Tears slipped from Mother's eyes. "Both men love us, but I can only have one son-in-law."

I stroked her hair. If Der was alive, Mother could have them both. "Who should be your son-in-law?" I asked.

"You and Kou are a perfect match, but we have to think about Nhia, too."

Nhia held the toy upside down and spun the wheels. He remembered everything Kou taught him. What a clever child! My priorities now were to raise him and care for my mother.

"Mother, I want to go to America as soon as possible. I'm worried about the Thai forcing us to go back, and I want a break from Kou and Pheng. I can't focus with them around."

"I'd love to have a man with us on the journey," she said.

Nhia pushed the toy on the floor.

"We have a man. This little guy is our man," I said.

"You are right," Mother smiled. "We have this little man, and I have you as the big man. I'm not afraid of anyone. I'm going to hold my head high. I'm ready to go to America."

My heart soared. "Thank you, Mother."

Chapter Thirty-Nine

My family arrived at the UNHCR building at ten a.m. Toua, Pa, and TouZou received a new BV. Mother, Nhia, and I got a separate one. It was sad to see the family divided into two, but it was the best way to deal with our different hopes for the future.

When Pheng arrived in midafternoon, I had him sit with me in the lean-to. Mother went to the market, Nhia was napping, and Toua and Pa were outside. I told Pheng about our new BV.

He scowled. "Why didn't you include me in this decision?"

"Let me explain. Der…." I paused, my gaze downcast. "My goal was to hand Nhia over to you, and help out sometimes, but that hasn't worked out. Nhia is a traumatized child. He needs good care, love, and patience. My mother and I are going to America. We can't leave him with you when he doesn't trust you. He needs to be with us until he feels safe. We must take him with us."

Pheng sighed. "I understand. I want to go with you. I don't want to separate from my son again."

"You are coming to America. It will be a short separation."

"You mentioned Der. What were you going to say?"

I hesitated. "Before Der died, she asked me to help raise Nhia. I'll try my best."

Pheng's face lit up. "Very clever of her. Der knew that you are the only one who would love Nhia as much as she and will meet his needs." His mouth quirked upwards. "Thanks to Der. Nhia needs you in his life."

He sounded like I had to marry him to meet Nhia's needs. I believed I could raise Nhia without marrying him. "My sister wanted the best for Nhia, that is why I'm taking him with me."

"Let's all go to the UNHCR office tomorrow to start our applications," he said.

"Yes. I heard the deadline is approaching."

"We have a few days. I'm going home to look for some documents and need to run a few errands. Meet me at eight a.m. tomorrow."

Later that evening, Kou visited, but after dinner I asked him to go home so I could study. After he left, I unfolded Father's paper and tried to read. I recognized a few words, but they didn't help me understand the message. I put the page back in the waist pouch to bring along in case the registrar asked for it.

In the morning, I whispered a quick prayer. "Father, Der, and grandparents, today is the day we're going to apply to go to America. May your spirits take away any obstacles we might encounter. Father, I'm going to register our little family as the family of a soldier. May your spirit guide me and make everything go smoothly."

We arrived at the UNHCR building before Pheng's family and were the first to go in. The registrar was Thai, and his Hmong interpreter sat next to him behind a wooden table.

"Hello, my name is Za. I am the interpreter," he said. "We'd like to see your BV."

Mother handed him the papers. The registrar studied the documents and looked us over. He talked to the interpreter.

Za said, "You are sixty-four years old."

"Yes," Mother said.

"Your daughter is sixteen and your grandson is only three."

"Yes."

"Where is your husband and this child's parents?" Za asked.

Mother told him that Father was a soldier, and he was killed during the trek through the jungle. Der was killed, and Nhia was born out of wedlock. I gave Father's paper to Za. He read and spoke to the registrar.

After their discussion, Za asked, "Do you have a sponsor in America?"

"No," said Mother.

I interrupted. "I know an American man named Edgar Buell or Than Pop. Can he be our sponsor?"

"I know him," Za said. "He's from America, but he lives in Bangkok, the capital city of Thailand. He can't be your sponsor."

Fear tightened my belly. "Can you find us a sponsor from America?"

"Yes."

Za and the registrar talked, and then the registrar left the room.

"He's going to check if Mr. Smith is available to talk to your family," said Za.

"Who is Mr. Smith?" I asked.

"He's one of the American interviewers. He decides who goes first, based on their situation. Your mother is old. According to the Americans, you are underage, and your nephew is very young. You'll likely be a high priority."

I looked at Mother with high hopes.

When the registrar returned, he spoke to Za.

Za said, "Mr. Smith is available at two p.m. this afternoon. Come back for your interview."

The registrar finished the application and put it away. I put

Nhia on my back and we walked outside. Pheng sat on the bench by the door. Many families were waiting in line.

He stood. "Sorry, we were late. How was it?"

"Super," I said with energy. "Our interview is at two this afternoon."

"So quick." He looked from Mother to me. "Oh, I understand. Because your mother is old and there is a child."

"According to the Americans, I'm a child, too," I said.

"Good." He nodded approval. "You will all probably get to leave before us."

"Where's your family?" I asked.

"My parents are inside. I don't need to be with them, so I waited for you."

Pheng came home with us. It was only nine o'clock. Though Za had skimmed Father's paper and told the registrar about it, Mr. Smith didn't yet know about Father's involvement in the war. I had to know what Father had written on the paper, so I could tell Mr. Smith.

Instead of making *paj ntaub,* I studied the paper and sounded out each word on the paper using the tones, vowels, and consonants that I'd learned. It took me a while to read all the words in the first sentence, but I was breathless when I read:

My name is Vang, Wa Shoua.

I recalled hearing Father say soldiers, students, and important people were called by their family names first followed by their given names. Regular people in the village addressed each other by their first names prefaced by uncle or aunt depending on the relationship.

Pheng watched me the whole time and smiled. I could ask him to read the paper for me, but that wouldn't teach me anything. Reading the paper was my way of learning. If I didn't get it done by the time of the interview, I'd ask Pheng to read the contents to me. I concentrated on my study.

Halfway through the front side, I began to grasp the concept of blending the consonants, vowels, and tones to make words. Pheng helped me when I struggled on certain words, but the reading got easier.

It took much time to read Father's paper, and I was filled with joy. I laughed heartily and squealed, "I can read! I can read!"

Pheng laughed with me. Mother, Pa, and Toua peeked in from outside the lean-to and smiled.

I wrote the important facts that I needed to know for the interview in my notebook:

Recruited in 1961. Was forty years old. CIA advisors were Jack Shirley and Tom Ahern and trainers were Thai PARU (Police Aerial Resupply Unit). Stationed at San Tiau, Lima Site 2. On April 19, the enemy attacked Site 2. Father was shot on the leg. Some soldiers were killed. Jack called for help and received ammunitions. The fight went on and more soldiers died. Jack, Tom and the remaining soldiers, including the wounded, fled. Air America helicopters found the group and rescued them. Father came home in 1962 due to his injury. He went to Long Chieng in 1966 and worked as a patrol officer. His leg continued to give him pain and he retired from the war and returned home in 1967.

Father was old when he joined the war. His injury meant no promotion, but it hadn't stopped him from serving his country. I was proud of my father. If he didn't get hurt, he'd have become a high-ranking officer. I wanted to know more about him working with the Americans and had many questions to ask him. Why did he have to die?

My father's dedication to his country made me think about my own. If he was alive, would he go back to Laos? Was Toua's refusal to go to America in line with Father's vision of protecting Laos?

. . .

At two o'clock, my family and I entered the interview room. Anxiety washed over me. Though we had a good chance, not everyone passed the interview. I didn't want to be one of the unlucky ones. The interviewer sat behind a desk and motioned for us to sit down in the chairs in front of his desk. He was old, about sixty, with wrinkles on his forehead. He was as white as sugar and his eyeglasses covered huge, blue eyes.

The interpreter was a different man. "I'm Cho Lee. I am the interpreter for Mr. Smith."

Mr. Smith asked a question.

Cho asked, "Why do you want to go to America?"

"The Communists killed my husband and daughter." Mother's voice wobbled. "They burned my village. We have to go to America for safety. My husband was a CIA soldier."

I gave Father's paper to Mr. Smith, and said, "This proves he worked for the CIA and was wounded in battle."

Cho translated and Mr. Smith gave him the paper. Then, Cho skimmed the paper and discussed it with Mr. Smith.

"Mr. Smith said your father is an important man," the interpreter said.

Pride filled me. "Yes," I said.

Cho and the American continued their discussion.

A few minutes later, Cho said, "Your family qualifies. St. Paul Catholic Church, the Diocese of Green Bay is the main sponsor, but the Johnson family from the church will be your sponsor and will take care of your family."

I held back a shout of joy. I wasn't a child anymore.

"They live in the city of Appleton, in the state of Wisconsin," the interpreter said.

Appleton, Wisconsin. "Can you write their names for me, please?" I asked.

Cho wrote the names on a piece of paper and gave it to me. "Now, you two stand up and take the oath."

Mother and I stood. Nhia remained on my back.

"Raise your right hand and repeat after Mr. Smith," he instructed.

We raised our hands and repeated, "I promise to be a good citizen in America."

"We'll schedule your family for a health screening next week," said Cho. "If you don't have any health issues, you'll be on your way to America."

"Can you tell us how we prepare for the screening?" I asked.

"There's nothing you can prepare for. The doctor will check your body to make sure you are healthy and don't have any diseases. The one thing that everyone complains about is being naked in front of the doctor."

My cheeks grew hot.

"Your appointment is ten o'clock on Thursday next week," Cho said.

Cho gave me the paper with the appointment written on it.

We left and found Pheng waiting outside. "How did it go?" he asked.

"We passed!" I shouted. "We took the oath! Our health screening is next week."

"Good." Sadness flashed across his face. "You'll leave me behind."

"But you're coming later," I said.

He gazed at Nhia, and Nhia buried his face in my shoulder. When would Nhia trust and accept his father? Would our separation further alienate him?

Chapter Forty

April 20, 1978

A warm, glowing sun spilled golden light upon the valley as we walked onto the dusty soccer field a month later. Five buses were parked parallel to each other in the middle. A crowd of people swarmed around us. My bus was the second one in line. It felt special to be the first group to leave, with other orphans and families who had seen tragedy. I had Nhia, Father's paper, and the Johnson family to thank.

The sound of cries echoed all around. Pheng, Kou, Toua, Pa, and Uncle Moua's family had all come to say goodbye.

"Please come to America." Mother stroked Toua's hair. "Don't stay here too long. Take good care of your family." She turned to Pa. "*Nyab,* I'll miss you. Be patient with Toua and keep telling him to come to America."

Pa nodded.

"I know you'll take good care of Mother and Nhia," Toua told me.

"I will," I said. "If you decide to come, I'll be your sponsor." I kissed TouZou who was asleep on Pa's back. "*Tis nyab,* sorry to leave you behind. I hope to support your family financially once we get there."

"Thank you," Pa said. "Be strong. You can do anything."

"Thank you," I replied.

Pheng's eyes were red from crying. I took Nhia to him.

"Give your father a hug. He's very sad that you are leaving him." Nhia shook his head. "Give your father a hug or I will not tell you stories and carry you. You'll have to walk for a long, long time. Do it."

Nhia leaned toward Pheng. Pheng hugged him and held him tight. Nhia started crying, and Pheng released him.

"We'll see you in America soon," I said.

"Yes." Pheng nodded. "As soon as I arrive in Minnesota, I'll come to get all of you from Wisconsin."

I faced Kou, who had remained quiet.

Tears filled his eyes as he handed me an envelope. "I wish you the best in America. Focus on your dreams."

I studied his face to remember every detail. I wished we were alone, so I could wipe his tears with my hands and hug him. The more I looked at him, the more it hurt to leave him. I blinked back tears.

"Your tears tell me that you care and will miss me," said Kou softly.

I nodded and wiped my eyes with my hand. "Please come to America."

"We will. Write to me."

"I will."

"Good-bye, young guardian." He smiled gently. "Take care of your mother and nephew. You are the most courageous girl I have ever met."

I couldn't help but smile. "Thanks for the title. I'll see you in America."

The officers ordered us to get on the bus. Mingled

murmurs turned to cries. The people's cries were louder than the bus engines.

"Yer, good-bye," I said.

"Good-bye. Write to me, too," Yer said.

"I will."

Pheng quickly smoothed Nhia's hair. "Be a good boy." He looked at me. "Good luck on your new journey. Be careful and take care." In my ear he whispered, "I love you with all my heart."

He tried hard to win my heart. The future was unknown. This separation would test Pheng, Kou, and me. It would test our hearts, our patience, and perhaps reveal true love.

Mother and I said our last farewells and got on the bus. The officers cleared the people on the ground. When everyone was seated, the bus moved slowly through the crowd. I waved good-bye through the window. Pheng, Kou, and Toua waved back.

I looked over my shoulder at Mother and smiled. She returned a grin. Next to me, I kissed Nhia on the forehead. My small family began our new journey. I couldn't believe I was on my way. I could have gone with Than Pop more than three years ago. If I had left with him, what would have happened to Mother, Nhia, Pa, and TouZou?

As we left the camp, I opened Kou's envelope and found a letter inside. I held the envelope against my chest. I loved him but leaving him would give me time to grow up, be independent, and focus on my dreams. If I studied hard and America was what I imagined, I might someday become a writer. Grandmother had blessed me for a good and prosperous life. I was confident that with her blessing and my determination, I would succeed.

I believed a bright future awaited me.

A Note From the Author

Why learn history? History helps us understand who we are, our roots, heritage, and identity. Everyone's family history is unique. We have all experienced hardship whether through the fight for equal rights, women's rights, natural disasters, wars, illness, immigration, or conflicts, before we find peace, safety, freedom, and prosperity.

The *Illiterate Daughter* is a work of fiction but is inspired by true events and contains real experiences of both my and my husband's family. My mother-in-law, who I consider my friend, told me stories that opened my eyes to my history. Why do I want to share these stories? Because these events shaped who we are today. I hope our stories give you insight into the Hmong's journey to freedom in the United States.

I will start with my family history. We begin in Laos, my country. My parents were farmers and life was peaceful before the Secret War. In order to stamp out communism in Southeast Asia, the United States started the Vietnam War in 1954. Soon after, the Secret War began in Laos, and the two wars continued until 1975.

Laos was declared a neutral state, which meant American

soldiers could fly planes and drop bombs, but they were prohibited from fighting on the ground. To counter this disadvantage, the United States recruited Hmong soldiers, including my father, to fight the communists on the ground. In the fifteen years of combat in my country, Laos, the US dropped more than two million tons of bombs. I was lucky not to be born yet because my mother and siblings fled for their lives, running from place to place while gunshots and bombs exploded around them.

When the United States withdrew from the Vietnam War and the Secret War in Laos, the Communists took over the countries and retaliated against those who fought with the Americans. Fear created a massive exodus out of Laos. My parents loved their homeland and refused to be displaced. For their safety, they hid in the jungles, and prayed for peace.

Because my father, Wa Tong Vang, was a former soldier for the Americans, the Communists hunted him down. This prolonged my family's time in hiding. A year living in the jungle of Laos seemed eternal. As I wrote in The Illiterate Daughter, there was little food. They foraged the jungle for anything to stave off hunger. The children suffered the most because they could eat very little wild grown food. In addition, the wound my father has sustained to his leg from fighting during the war gave him great pain.

With no other choice, my father risked his life and took us back to a village. On this leg of their perilous journey, I was born on the hillside of a mountain. With a newborn to care for, little strength and no rest, the journey almost killed my mother. She fought hard to save herself and me because without her and what little milk her body could give me, I would die. Being born a healthy baby helped me survive. My family made it to a village. Our father left us there, then disappeared back to the jungle, leaving his wife and six children to survive on their own. My mother worked the fields tirelessly to feed us.

After a few months in the jungle, my father escaped to Thailand with other former soldiers. Once a year, he sneaked back into Laos to see us. After a few years, the Hmong spies discovered his visits and alerted the Communists. He stopped visiting. My younger brother and I grew up not knowing our father. After my oldest brother married, the Communists threatened to arrest him if my father didn't return and surrender. My father's dream to return and live in peace in his homeland was shattered. He had no choice but to bring his family to Thailand.

One day my father returned to our village in Laos and instructed us to leave with him. My mother and older siblings packed clothes and food in their backpacks and rattan baskets, and our family of ten left that evening. The only family who knew of our departure was our neighbor, my uncle's family. My uncle could have left with us but, like my father, he didn't want to leave his homeland and the risk was high.

We traveled ten days on foot through the rugged mountain paths. My father knew the safest route to travel. Even with his experience and knowledge, we still took great precautions and trekked at night in areas heavily patrolled by the enemy or when we passed near Communist villages. My niece was two years old, and she sometimes cried. For the family's safety, my brother and sister-in-law quieted her with small doses of opium which, if given in too high a dose, can easily kill a child.

My family of ten made it to the Mekong River and we waited in the jungle until dark. We couldn't swim, so my father had hired two men to help take us cross the wide river. He tied a rope from two of his children's waists to each of the swimmers and strapped a plastic tube to each child. My father tied his rope to my mother's waist. My mother carried my younger brother on her back while my father carried me on his back with his backpack. We reached the Thai shore.

My husband's family faced even greater challenges during the war and trek to freedom than us. Here is their history.

During the Secret War while fleeing for safety, my mother-in-law lost her five-year-old twin son and daughter to illness. Without a son, her life was shattered. She had given birth to four other sons and three daughters who she left behind with her first husband's family after he died, and she remarried. Those sons also died. The birth of my husband, Pao Lee, brought her hope because boys are priceless in our culture. But constant fear and the challenge to survive tested them daily. This was a horrible time to grow up. Gunfire and his family's constant fleeing in the middle of the night frightened the young Pao. Out of fear, he learned not to cry.

After the Secret War, Pao's family sought safety in several villages. The unstable life left the family no choice but to surrender and settle in a Communist village. Guards from a nearby military camp harassed the villagers year round. The ongoing arrest and killing of former soldiers and their families incited even more fear and soon many people disappeared.

A group planned to escape and Pao's family joined the pack of about two hundred escapees of various ages. During the journey, opium was administered to crying children, and whispering and body language was the adults' main communication methods. But these precautions weren't enough, as they couldn't hide the tracks of such a large group. They were caught, and the unfortunate ones were shot while the strong and fortunate scattered. Luckily, Pao's family was unharmed and reunited with other families.

The new group was trapped for a few days and decided to continue on the journey instead of returning to the village to face the Communist's Pathet Lao. Desperate to reach safety in Thailand, the group paid smugglers to escort them. But these escorts deserted them at a mountain that separated them from the Mekong River, which divides Laos and Thailand. Pao's family needed to cross the Communist village in the valley to the river without being detected. Night was their only hope. They waited until dark and moved swiftly like ghosts around the village and down to the river.

Suddenly, gunshots burst around them and once again the group fled for their lives. Darkness made it difficult to track the family. Seven-year-old Pao trembled on his mother's back and clutched her tightly as she ran to the jungle where the trees shielded them.

When daylight came, Pao's mother found her grandson and daughter-in-law, who was nine months pregnant. They searched for survivors and found a family of three, a mother and two young girls. They stayed together and feared for their missing family members.

It was December, the dry season, and the two families searched for food in vain. People from Thailand would risk their lives by searching the Laos side of the Mekong River for refugees. The family waited near the Mekong River for someone to arrive in a canoe to rescue them, but no one came. Pao's sister-in-law went into labor and gave birth to a lovely baby boy. The family was unable to keep the infant warm in the cold weather and he cried often. Afraid for their lives, Pao's mother gave the child opium to quiet him. The tiny body couldn't tolerate the drug and he died.

Starvation and fear haunted the two families. Pao's mother watched for a canoe by the shore. After two days, one came. The family reached Thailand and reunited with Pao's older brother and young niece who had swam across the Mekong River the night of the attack.

A week later, the family learned that Pao's father, sister, and aunt were caught the night they were separated and were taken to a village as prisoners. Starvation and illness killed Pao's sister before his father and aunt managed to escape a month later.

After a year, Pao's father and aunt joined a group that escaped to Thailand. At last, the family was reunited.

Pao's family arrived in Ban Vinai Refugee Camp in Thailand three years before my family arrived. Our stay in the camp overlapped theirs, but we weren't destined to meet there. Both families were hesitant to go to a third country and stayed in the crowded, stinky camp for six years. Both families believed there would be peace in Laos and wanted to return one day. The dream to return to live safely and peacefully diminished and the pressure from family members induced our two families to immigrate to the United States.

My family settled in Appleton, Wisconsin. My husband's family came to Eau Claire, Wisconsin. My husband and I were teenagers at the time. We didn't know each other. One day Pao visited his uncle in Appleton, and the uncle told him about me. In the small Hmong community in Appleton, the adults knew everyone. His uncle knew my family. Shortly after we met, we married.

Many Hmong families went through similar experiences as our two families, and I decided to write *The Young Guardian* series to teach our youth about the Hmong's journey to freedom and why we came to the United States. We were forced to leave our country because we fought on behalf of the United States. Many Hmong soldiers and families died for our freedom.

I hope *The Young Guardian* series inspires you to dig into your family history and share it with the world, because history is a preservation of the past for future generations to understand who they are.

Dreamer's Dream

After their harrowing escape from Communist-held Laos, seventeen-year-old Nou Vang immigrates to America with her disabled mother and traumatized three-year-old nephew. None of them speak English, so Nou can only nod and smile at the American sponsors who meet them at the airport.

When their sponsor's son, Peter, offers to teach Nou English, she grabs this chance to overcome the final barrier to her dream of an education. As her proficiency with the foreign language grows, so too does her love for Peter and her confidence in being able to care for her family in a country free of war.

While Peter can help her learn English and enroll in school, her American sponsors are helpless when her mother falls ill and refuses to see an American doctor. When Nou's mother demands Hmong rituals in order to recover, Nou turns to the shaman of the small, local Hmong community. But the shaman's son, Xa, becomes infatuated with Nou and begins testing her as a potential wife.

In addition to dealing with bullies who throw eggs and shout at her to "Go home," Nou must now handle this new threat to her freedom—a marriage proposal supported by her mother and the Hmong community. Fearful of doing anything that might get her family expelled from America, Nou struggles with the clash of American and Hmong cultures. However, when Xa kidnaps her with the intention of forcing her to marry him, Nou faces the likelihood of losing her dream just when she thought she was safe.

www.scarsdalepublishing.com

Made in the USA
Columbia, SC
08 November 2022